D0344330

Just Be Cool, Jenna Sakai

ALSO BY DEBBI MICHIKO FLORENCE

Keep It Together, Keiko Carter

Just Be Cool, Jenna Sakai

BY DEBBI MICHIKO FLORENCE

Scholastic Press / New York

Library of Congress Cataloging-in-Publication Data

Names: Florence, Debbi Michiko, author.
Title: Just be cool, Jenna Sakai / Debbi Michiko Florence.
Description: First edition. | New York : Scholastic Inc., 2021. | Audience: Ages 8-12. | Audience: Grades 4-6. | Summary: When boyfriend Elliot breaks up with Jenna Sakai before Christmas break, she just about convinces herself that relationships are for suckers and she is better off without them; but unfortunately she finds herself in competition with Elliot for a journalism scholarship, and worse her first assignment for the newspaper club is to write a personal essay, which is difficult when you are someone who prefers to keep your emotions bottled up—and then there is Rin Watanabe, a boy as stubborn as Jenna herself, and a mystery that Jenna cannot help but investigate.
Identifiers: LCCN 2020043874 (print) | LCCN 2020043875 (ebook) | ISBN 9781338671568 (hardcover) | ISBN 9781338671582 (ebk)
Subjects: LCSH: Japanese Americans—Juvenile fiction. | Dating (Social customs)—Juvenile fiction. | Interpersonal relations—Juvenile fiction. | Self-perception—Juvenile fiction. | Best friends—Juvenile fiction. | Student newspapers and periodicals—Juvenile fiction. | CYAC: Japanese Americans—Fiction. | Dating (Social customs)—Fiction. | Self-perception—Fiction. | Best friends—Fiction. | Friendship—Fiction. | Newspapers—Fiction. | Middle schools—Fiction. | Schools—Fiction.
Classification: LCC PZ7.1.F593 Ju 2021 (print) | LCC PZ7.1.F593 (ebook) | DDC 813.6 [Fic]—dc23
LC record available at https://lccn.loc.gov/2020043874
LC ebook record available at https://lccn.loc.gov/2020043875

1 2021

Printed in the U.S.A.   23
First edition, August 2021

Book design by Stephanie Yang

To Lynn Bauer, anam cara,
for always being on my side

one

Heartbreak is for suckers.

Smart people protected their hearts, and I wasn't stupid. Far from it. I locked my heart in a vault and buried it where nobody could trample on it. Which was why even though Elliot Oxford dumped me right before Christmas break, my heart was still whole.

Two weeks later, I'd made it through the entire first day back at school without any mention of Elliot. My best friend, Keiko Carter, hadn't brought him up once. She'd texted me while I was at my dad's in Texas for the holidays to see if I was okay. But I didn't answer. And after several long, "meaningful" looks from her at lunch, it looked like she'd taken the hint. Now all I had to do was avoid Elliot at newspaper club. It wasn't as if we *had* to work together. Ignoring him was going to be a piece of cake.

Unfortunately, I ran into Elliot on the way to my locker after school. And I mean literally.

I rounded a corner too quickly in my rush to get to Ms. Fontes's classroom, and Elliot and I crashed into each other. My messenger bag slipped off my shoulder and thudded to the ground. We both leaned down to reach for it at the same time and knocked heads.

"Ow!" I straightened and rubbed my forehead.

"It was an accident," Elliot said, handing me my bag. I snatched it from him. He was the last person I wanted to talk to.

His eyes traveled over me. "You cut your hair. And colored it."

"Way to state the obvious," I grumbled. I tugged the shorter turquoise strands. While I often dyed my hair when I was upset, this time I'd just wanted a fresh start: new year, new shade. Or at least that's what I'd told myself.

"Right." Elliot pressed his mouth into a straight line.

I hefted my bag onto my shoulder as we stood there awkwardly.

"Are you heading to newspaper club?" he asked.

"Why? Did you hope I'd drop it?"

Elliot frowned. I used to think that furrow between his eyebrows was cute. Not anymore. "Why do you have to be so angry all the time?" he asked.

"Why can't you stop judging people?"

"It's not judgment. It's observation. A great journalist is a great observer. You should know that."

Oh, he was going to go there again? "A great journalist is also objective."

"Something you can't be if you're shooting angry flames out of your eyes all the time."

"That's physically impossible," I snapped.

"That's called a metaphor," Elliot said calmly.

Gah! I hated when he got all condescending. I decided to skip my locker. I pivoted and stalked to newspaper club. Alone. The way I liked it.

I swooped into the room and took a quick look around. Ms. Fontes, our sponsor, wasn't here yet. She always ran out for a coffee after school but left the door unlocked for the rest of us. I counted seven, so only Elliot was missing.

Passing the table I used to share with Elliot, I made my way to the opposite end of the room and sat next to Isabella Baker.

"Hey," she said. She wore gold eye shadow that sparkled against her dark brown skin. "Oh! I love your hair!"

"Thanks." I smiled.

"Did you have a good break?"

"Pretty good." I'd spent the entire two weeks at my dad's. My first Christmas away from home, without both of my parents together. At least the weather in Texas hadn't been too different from Southern California. "How was yours?"

"Stellar! My sister came home from college, and she helped me with my fashion designs." Isabella's eyes flitted behind me. "Where's Elliot?"

Oh. I'd forgotten about this part. I'd have to actually tell people we broke up. "I'm not sure," I said.

"There he is!"

I turned, and yep, there he was. He strolled in, and when I saw him this time, from a distance without him right in my face, I was able to check him out. He wore a blue-and-green plaid button-down with cargo pants and Vans. His chestnut-brown hair was, as usual, a little long, but I'd liked it like that. It always smelled like coconut and was so soft. My chest tightened. I'd never touch his hair again. I quickly swung back around in my seat.

Isabella made a small sound when Elliot sat across the room at our old table.

"Are you two fighting?" she whispered.

I liked Isabella. I admired her writing style and fashion sense. We both favored T-shirts with sayings and bold graphics. Today mine was the Sandra Oh quote IT'S AN HONOR JUST TO BE ASIAN, while Isabella wore her BIG IS BEAUTIFUL shirt. Except while I paired my tees with jeans, she usually wore hers with colorful skirts.

It was better to come clean. As Keiko always said, rip that Band-Aid off.

"We broke up," I said at a normal volume.

Isabella gasped. Caitlin and Laurel at the next table glanced at me and then at Elliot. I followed their gaze. He was talking with Carlos and Thea, who usually sat with us. Him. *Sat with him*, I mentally corrected.

"What happened?" Isabella asked. She had that same concerned look Keiko had had when I told her the news the day before I'd left for my dad's. "You two were so perfect together."

Perfect? There was no such thing. I'd made a big mistake with Elliot, thinking our relationship would work because he was cute and we both wanted to be writers. Relationships were a waste of time. Look at my parents. They'd bragged about their meet-cute storybook romance, had a Hawaiian destination wedding, and celebrated their anniversaries with extravagant gifts. Sixteen years and a billion arguments later, they got a divorce.

Fortunately, Ms. Fontes walked into the room just then, holding her giant reusable mug of iced coffee. I was relieved not to have to continue the conversation with Isabella but also glad to have it out in the open. Maybe then nobody else would ask about Elliot.

"Good afternoon, reporters!" Ms. Fontes smiled and leaned against her desk. "Last semester you learned the aspects of putting together a newspaper. Researching, interviewing, writing, revising, and also design, layout, and production. This semester I'm going to push you out of your comfort zones. Your first assignment will be to try out an area of journalism you haven't necessarily gravitated toward in the past. And it's due on my desk next Thursday. I know that's not a lot of time, but to put out a paper, you will need to learn to work fast. And yes, I'm aware that we aren't actually putting out a paper. This club is all about learning so when you get to high school, you'll be ready for the real thing." Ms. Fontes looked down at her notebook and started calling out assignments.

"Elliot, sports."

I held in a snicker. I definitely knew more about sports than Elliot. Most people knew more about sports than Elliot. This was going to be entertaining.

"Ben, you'll handle the Pacific Vista beat, covering school announcements. Caitlin, write an article, any topic, at least two hundred and fifty words long."

Caitlin tapped her pencil against her sketchbook. She was our resident photographer and artist.

Ms. Fontes continued. "Thea, you write great movie reviews. Try a book review or two. Brody, instead of the sports page, give me an opinion piece. And it can't be your opinion of the Super Bowl."

Everyone laughed, including Brody, who gave Ms. Fontes two thumbs-up.

"Carlos, try your hand at a profile of the new science teacher, Ms. Shah."

Carlos, the only eighth grader in our club made up of seventh graders, scribbled in his notebook. He, Elliot, and I usually wrote feature articles. I focused on environmental and cultural issues while he and Elliot wrote mostly about local and school news.

"Jenna"—Ms. Fontes nodded at me—"I'd like to see you write a personal essay."

A loud rushing of air filled my ears. Personal essay? I pondered the words like they were a foreign language. Personal essay. Personal. Essay. What was the point of writing something like that for a newspaper? Personal essays were all about feelings and little stories and other useless stuff. They weren't news. And writing about feelings would mean, well, feeling them. There was no point. I was all about facts and objectivity. That's why I wanted to be a reporter!

I was so lost in my head that I missed the rest of the assignments.

I turned to Isabella. "What did you get?" She

usually wrote about fashion, music, and pop culture.

She sighed. "Feature article, investigative piece."

That was an assignment that would have been perfect for me. "Any ideas about what you'll work on?"

Isabella shook her head, her dark curls bouncing. "You?"

I rolled my eyes. "I don't know that I've ever seen a personal essay in a newspaper."

"Sure you have. Like those Modern Love essays in the *New York Times*."

"The what?"

Isabella smiled. "My mom loves them. Essays written by everyday people about their experiences with love and hope."

I jiggled my leg. That sounded horrible and *way* too personal. But I didn't say so to Isabella. "Hmm," I said instead. "I don't think I've ever seen those."

"Look them up. Some of them are pretty amazing," she said. "Now, help me figure out what I should investigate."

I nodded. "If it were my assignment, I'd look into where the funds came from to renovate our cafeteria over the summer. I mean, have you seen it? It's super fancy. I heard one anonymous donation covered the whole thing. It had to have been huge. And the old cafeteria was fine. I mean, why not use the money for something more important, like updating our computers or remodeling our sad library?" Or funding a real school newspaper.

"Oooh! Good idea!" Isabella scribbled on her paper, then stopped. "Except you meant that as an example."

I shrugged. "It's a good angle, and it's not like I'll get to write it. Go ahead. And if you want help..." I let the rest of the sentence go unsaid.

Isabella raised her eyebrows. "Really?"

"Yeah, yeah, I know. Shocking." Elliot and I had quite a reputation for being competitive and secretive about our articles. It had gotten so heated that Ms. Fontes started assigning us articles to work on together to teach us teamwork and how to cowrite.

"Okaaaaay," Isabella said, dragging out the word like she was afraid I'd take it back.

"You'll do great," I said. "Look for an original angle. Try to find out from the office staff who the donor was. Even if it was anonymous, someone has to know where the money came from."

"Thanks, Jenna! And seriously, read some of those Modern Love essays. The writing is great, and they're from a world-renowned paper, so you know they're the real deal."

"Right." I glanced at Ms. Fontes, who was engrossed in a conversation with Elliot. I still thought personal essays did not belong in a paper. It made zero sense. I would talk to her on Wednesday and get her to give me a different assignment.

I was an excellent student, and Ms. Fontes knew it. I was sure she'd totally be okay with me doing something else.

two

When I got home that afternoon, Keiko was waiting on my front porch. Most days after school, she played basketball with her boyfriend, Conner Lassiter, and his friends Doug Nolan and Teddy Chen at the park. Usually after that, she and Conner walked their dogs, but since we hadn't hung out just the two of us since before Christmas break, she'd promised to come to my house today. It was nice to have some time alone with her.

We headed straight to my room, where we had to step over piles of dirty clothes, books, my mostly unpacked suitcase, and pens scattered across the floor.

I threw myself onto my unmade bed and stared up at the ceiling. Keiko sat down next to me, surveying the disaster. The navy-blue quilt shoved to the foot of my mattress was not unusual. The stuff all over the floor was. Keiko knew better than to comment, but I could read the question on her face.

"It's not what you think," I said, sitting up next to her.

She turned to me. "And what do I think?"

"That this"—I waved my hand at my floor—"is because of Elliot."

"It's not?"

"No!" I softened my voice. "I'm fine."

"Jenna," she said. "It's only been two weeks. You're allowed to be upset."

I grabbed my teddy bear—the one my dad had won for me at the county fair before he and Mom got divorced last year—and squeezed it to my chest.

Keiko gently took the bear out of my chokehold. "You know you can always talk to me."

I sighed loudly. The thing was, I wasn't upset. "I know. But I'm telling you, I'm fine."

"You haven't talked about the breakup at all." She frowned. "At least not with me."

It wasn't like I had anyone else to talk to. "Like I said, I'm fine."

Because Keiko was my best friend, she didn't argue. Instead she asked, "You want help cleaning up?"

I tossed dirty clothes into the laundry basket in the closet while Keiko stacked my books back on the shelf, in alphabetical order by author's last name. She knew me well. Just as I closed my closet door, Keiko's phone chimed with a familiar text tone.

I glanced at her, but Keiko continued straightening my books.

"You can look at your phone, you know," I said. "Seriously, Keiko, I promise you, I'm not that kind of fragile and you know it. Tell Conner I say hey."

Conner and Keiko had gotten together a few weeks after Elliot and I had, but unlike me and Elliot, they'd been friends for years before. And they were still together.

Keiko smiled as she read the message and then dashed off a quick response. She glanced up at me, an overly concerned look crossing her face.

"Keiko," I said, my voice a warning. "I'm not a kid anymore. This isn't my parents' divorce. It was a middle school relationship. It's not a big deal. No offense."

She studied me a bit longer. I plastered a smile on my face.

"Okay," she said. "But I'm here for you if you want to talk."

I turned to empty out the rest of my suitcase. Talking didn't help anything. During my parents' divorce, I'd talked and talked to Keiko. Until Audrey—Conner's sister, who used to be our other best friend—would join us. She was so judgmental, I hadn't wanted to talk in front of her. So I'd go dead silent. And I'd learned a valuable lesson. Not talking about it was better. I didn't have to think about the divorce or feel anything. Not talking about it meant I could forget about it. And I intended to deal with Elliot the same way.

"You really want to help?" I asked. Keiko nodded her head so hard I was surprised it didn't fall off. "Then can you get the shredder from my mom's room?"

While Keiko went to grab it, I turned up my computer speakers and blasted P!nk, which I'd been playing on repeat the entire holiday break.

When Keiko returned, rolling the shredder in front of her, I grabbed a small purple shoebox from under my bed. The loud music kept Keiko from asking any questions. She was smart. She'd figure out what I was doing without us having to talk.

As Keiko sat down next to me on the floor, I took a deep breath, opened the box, and riffled through the contents: articles Elliot and I had worked on together in newspaper club, a card for our one-month anniversary, receipts from meals we'd had together. I had the business card from the coffee shop we'd gone to on our first date, and a cardboard coaster from Islands, the restaurant where we'd shared a guacamole burger and fries for our one-month anniversary.

Without a word, Keiko plugged in the shredder. I handed her the stack of paper, and she fed it into the machine, destroying everything. I wished I could shred my memories into oblivion.

I pulled out the scarf I'd bought but hadn't given Elliot for Christmas. It was green and yellow, his favorite colors. Keiko held out her hand. I shook my head. It wouldn't go through the shredder. But I didn't want to keep it, either. Keiko gave me a meaningful look and shook her open hand at me again. I blew out a breath and handed it over. Then she stood and bolted out of my room with it. I figured she'd gone to dump it in the trash can in the garage.

I glanced into the box, which wasn't quite empty. At the bottom was the pen Elliot had let me use in newspaper club and said I could keep. I picked it up and twirled it. It had great balance and smooth ink. I'd keep this. It wasn't as if a person could be sentimental over a pen.

I quickly shoved it into my messenger bag just as Keiko returned, empty-handed. She reached over and turned down the volume of the music.

"Let's talk, Jenna," she said, sitting on my bed.

"There's nothing to talk about."

"I thought we didn't keep secrets from each other." Keiko left out the "anymore," but it was implied.

The whole friendship bust-up with Audrey happened because I hadn't come clean about having a crush on Elliot. I hadn't meant for it to be a secret, but when Audrey had announced she liked Elliot at the start of seventh grade and intended to make him her boyfriend, I froze. When it came out that Elliot and I were already kind of a thing, Audrey lost it and acted like I'd betrayed her or something. In the end, she'd done much worse to Keiko, but I still felt burned.

"I'm not keeping secrets," I said. "I just don't need to pick the whole thing apart."

"Okay," she said without much conviction. "I'm here if you need me."

"Oh my God, Keiko," I said, my voice rising. "I heard you! You said that a million times already. I'm fine! I don't need to talk about it!"

Keiko blinked and then busied herself with smoothing out the blankets on my bed.

I sighed. She didn't deserve my bad attitude. She had always been there for me. Always. And she's never judged me.

"So, hey," I said. "This semester, newspaper club only meets Mondays, Wednesdays, and Fridays. We can hang out after school on Tuesdays and Thursdays."

Keiko smiled.

"I know you go to Conner's basketball games on Tuesdays. We can watch together," I said. "And I can go with you to the games you play with them. Don't make me play, though."

"On Thursdays, let's just do stuff the two of us," Keiko said. "I don't need to play every day."

"But what about Conner?"

She shook her head. "I see him all the time. I want to hang out with you."

I finally smiled.

"And you can come to family game night at my house on Saturdays."

"That would be fun." I hadn't been to game night since before the divorce.

"Be warned, though," Keiko said. "My mom has gotten super competitive. I swear she's going to make Doug and Teddy cry one of these days." Keiko laughed.

I hadn't realized that all the guys had been going to game night at Keiko's. I felt a twinge of something. Like I was on the outside looking in.

"And you'll eat lunch with us, right? It was nice having you there today." Keiko squeezed my arm. "This is going to be awesome, Jenna! I'm so glad we're hanging out!"

I was, too. And it was all because Elliot and I had broken up.

It was for the best. Now I could focus on what was really important. School. Friends. Newspaper club. Someday, I wanted to be a top-notch investigative journalist. That meant I needed to be objective and dedicated. I had to avoid any stupid emotional distractions. Be a little heartless.

I could do that.

three

At lunch the next day, I made my way to the bleachers by the gym. Keiko and the guys were clustered at the top two rows. She laughed as she handed a bag of chips to Conner, while his best friends, Doug and Teddy, were deep in conversation.

I hesitated, clutching my lunch bag. I'd started seventh grade eating lunch with Keiko and Audrey. But then Audrey became more of a drama queen than usual and I couldn't deal anymore. Keiko stayed, but I started spending my lunch periods with Elliot in Ms. Fontes's room. Then Audrey had stopped hanging out, and Conner and the boys had taken her place. I didn't want to insert myself where I didn't belong. It was obvious that Keiko and the guys were a solid group.

I realized now that spending all that time with Elliot had been stupid. I'd left myself wide open and vulnerable by allowing myself to get attached. I would not be making that mistake again. Not with boys. Not with anyone.

It wasn't like Keiko and I had stopped being friends, but things weren't the same as before. I looked around. Maybe I could eat alone. I wouldn't need to rely on anyone. I could just be that chill, serious loner. In fact, the more I thought about it, the more perfect that felt. But where could I go to get away from everyone?

"Jenna! Over here!"

Keiko's voice carried. She stood and waved both arms at me. I couldn't miss that. I squared my shoulders, walked over to the bleachers, and climbed to the top. She patted the seat next to her.

Just as I sat, Doug leaned toward me. "Dude, what superpower would *you* have?"

"First off," I said, "I'm no dude."

Doug shrugged.

Keiko nudged me. "They have these ridiculous conversations all the time. It's always better just to humor them."

"Ha-ha! That's how we get you..." Teddy turned to Doug and Conner. "You guys are wrong. Invisibility is *totally* superior to mind reading."

"I'm glad you're here," Keiko said to me.

As I took a big bite of my sandwich, I realized I was glad I was here, too.

"I hear you're coming to our game today," Conner said to me.

I nodded as I chewed.

"Excellent!" Doug clapped once. "Our cheering section has doubled!"

The guys laughed. They were doofuses, but at least they weren't jerks anymore. All last year, they had tormented me, Keiko, and Audrey. The ridiculous name-calling hadn't bothered me as much as it had Audrey and Keiko, but all the same, this was much better, and I actually found myself looking forward to watching the guys' basketball game.

After last-period PE, Keiko and I walked to the park. When we got there, I was surprised to see how crowded it was. All six courts had players, and there seemed to be official timekeepers.

"They have refs?" I asked Keiko.

"It's a league organized by the park."

"Oh." I hadn't realized it was a real thing.

I followed Keiko to the benches in front of the court where Conner, Doug, and Teddy were warming up. And then I stopped in my tracks.

"What?" Keiko turned to look at me. She saw my face and scanned the crowd. "Oh."

Elliot was sitting in the third row.

I stalked over to him. "What are you doing here?"

His eyes grew wide. "What are *you* doing here?"

"I asked you first." Seriously! What was Elliot Oxford doing at a three-on-three basketball game at the park?

Elliot rolled his eyes and closed the notebook on his lap. "I'm doing my assignment for Ms. Fontes. I'm supposed to be writing about sports, remember?"

"And you're covering a park league? It's not even part of our school!"

"I wanted a new angle. Every sports article we do is about one of our teams at school." Elliot nodded at the court. "Teddy Chen is in my PE class. He told me about the league.

He and the rest of his team go to PV Middle, so it's still school-related. How's your essay coming along?"

Gah! Why couldn't he mind his own business? And did he have to cover the league today? He didn't care at all how my essay was coming along. The only thing he cared about was being the best. Or at least being better than me.

I swung around without answering and rejoined Keiko, who waited for me on the sidelines.

"Do you want to go somewhere else?" she asked. "We don't have to stay."

I flopped onto the bench and jiggled my leg. "We're staying." Elliot wasn't going to chase me off.

Keiko sat down, watching me. I sighed and turned to her. "I'm okay. Please stop tiptoeing around my feelings. It's starting to annoy me."

Hurt flashed across Keiko's face, and for a quick moment, I felt bad. But maybe now she'd back off.

Soon the game had started, and Keiko was too busy cheering for Conner and the guys to hover over me. I tried hard to pay attention. I usually loved watching basketball, and though it was no Bruins game, it was pretty entertaining. But I was distracted, wondering how Elliot was following the action. We'd watched two college games on TV, and he'd been completely bored and confused. He totally didn't get the rules. That had been the last time we'd watched sports together.

Mostly we hung out at school in Ms. Fontes's classroom after newspaper club was over. We'd play this silly interview game, kind of like twenty questions.

"Favorite food?" I'd asked early on.

"Fried chicken sandwich," Elliot said. "You?"

"Japanese curry."

"Isn't all curry the same?"

"No. Japanese curry uses less spices than Indian curry and is more like stew than gravy." I leaned back in my chair. "Now I'm hungry."

"What do you like about it?"

"What do you mean?"

Elliot leaned forward, his eyes bright like whenever he got really excited about something. "For me, the fried chicken sandwich makes me think of visiting my grandparents. My grandpa makes the best fried chicken ever, and it reminds me of eating on his porch and playing cards every summer. I mean, the sandwich is definitely outstanding, but for me, it's more about my grandpa."

"Oh. Well, I guess I just love curry because it's thick and delicious and served over rice."

That wasn't entirely true. Japanese curry *was* sentimental for me. It was Dad's favorite meal. But after he left, Mom pretty much tossed out anything remotely associated with him, including family traditions. Curry Sunday dinners went right out the door, along with my dad.

"Oh," Elliot had said with a disappointed frown and a cute furrow between his brows.

The interviews he and I did with each other had been fun, at least until he got all competitive.

"Your last two questions were a little basic," he'd said a month into it.

"What are you talking about?"

"You need to dig deeper. Like I do."

I shook my head. "I thought we were only playing. You know, getting to know each other."

"I'm just saying if you want to be a great reporter, you might as well use every opportunity to improve your skills, right?"

I'd tried a little harder after that, but the fun had gone out of it. Elliot was supersmart and ambitious, and I admired him for it, but sometimes it got annoying. He liked to be right about everything. In fact, the main reason we'd stopped watching basketball together was that he hated that I knew more about it than he did.

A whistle blast shook me out of my thoughts. Conner had gotten fouled.

It would be funny to see Elliot's face all scrunched in confusion. He probably wondered why Conner was getting a free throw. I turned to look at Elliot, but he wasn't watching Conner. He was watching me. My heart slammed into my throat, and I quickly swung back around.

"I have to go," I told Keiko in a rush. I didn't give her a chance to object—I just grabbed my bag and fled from the courts. I knew I was being rude, but I couldn't stick around the park for a second longer.

I wanted to forget Elliot, and that was impossible when he was everywhere I looked.

four

Now that I wasn't spending the afternoon at the game, I had some time to kill. With tax season coming up, Mom was getting busier and wouldn't be home from the accounting firm till well after six. And I definitely was in too foul a mood to go home. I'd just stew about Elliot. I needed a distraction.

So I left the park the back way and started walking without any real purpose. I spotted Passages, a tiny bookstore I loved, ahead but couldn't bring myself to stop. Elliot and I had browsed there together. Great. He'd ruined one of my favorite places to hang out.

I turned left onto Beach Boulevard and ended up in

an area I hadn't been to before. It was mostly industrial complexes, but across the street was an old-fashioned diner. The sign, faded and battered, read LEIGH'S STAGE DINER. I wasn't sure it was open. The teal paint was chipped, and the sidewalk in front buckled from past earthquakes. I crossed the street and peered in a smudged window. There were customers inside.

I texted my mom to let her know I'd left the park. Ever since the divorce, her rules had gotten...loose. I only had to check in regularly after school and let her know where I was. She texted back a thumbs-up and reminded me to be home before dark.

I walked up a cement ramp, and when I pushed open the glass door, a bell tied to the inside handle tinkled. For how run-down the outside of the place looked, the inside was spotless. The vintage black-and-white-tiled floor sparkled. Red-cushioned stools lined a long counter edged in shiny chrome. Against the opposite wall with big picture windows stood booths with wood benches, the tables topped with white-and-black-speckled laminate that matched the counter. It was oddly quiet for a diner. No music played. That was kind of nice.

"Sit wherever you want, honey," a waitress with red glasses called from behind the cash register.

I passed an old man reading the paper at the counter and two moms with toddlers in a booth as I walked to the back of the diner and tucked myself into the far corner booth. It was the largest one. Maybe I should have saved it for a big group, but the waitress said to sit wherever I wanted and I doubted a big crowd would be showing up any time soon. After sliding all the way in and dumping my bag next to me, I pulled out my newspaper club notebook. In case inspiration struck.

And there was a lot to be inspired by. The diner was decorated with posters for Broadway shows. I recognized a few. One was for *Waitress*, which was maybe too spot-on. But funny. I also noticed posters for *Newsies*, *Rent*, and *Fiddler on the Roof*. I liked the theme. It had personality.

I snagged a plastic-coated menu and perused. I expected pages of every typical diner item possible but instead found a short list of sandwiches and salads on the front and side dishes and beverages on the back. The menu items had long strange names: Jean Valjean's Stolen Garlic Bread, the Welcome Home to

Santa Fe Salad, and the Phantom of the Onion Burger.

My stomach rumbled. I glanced at the chalkboard over the counter for the daily specials. They had milkshakes! And the flavors also had weird names like Lulu's Strawberry Dream Pie, Grape Jellicle, Banana and the Beast, and Rum Raisin in the Sun.

"All the ice cream for the shakes is made in-house," the waitress who'd greeted me said as she approached my booth. "I'm Leigh. Owner, manager, waitress, and cashier. My husband, Tom, is the chef."

"Um, hi. I'm Jenna."

Leigh smiled and nodded at the menu. "I recommend the cheesy fries and the *Waitress* shake, made with roasted strawberry ice cream."

Waitress shake? What did that mean? I glanced down at the menu to check out the fries. Regina George's Fetch Fries with Cheese. I wrinkled my nose.

"You don't like fries?" Leigh asked.

"I like fries. I'm just confused about these names."

Leigh laughed. "Not a Broadway fan?"

Ah, that made sense. Regina George was from *Mean Girls*. I remembered seeing the old movie on DVD with Keiko and Audrey.

"Each booth is named, too," Leigh said, tapping a small plaque at the front of the table. "You're in the *Hamilton* booth."

I stared at the small brass sign under Leigh's finger, even though it was too small for me to read. "I saw that show," I said. "In LA."

"Same! Amazing, right?" Leigh nodded. "So, what can I get you?"

"Um, the things you recommended sound good."

"Fetch Fries with Cheese and a *Waitress* shake! You got it!"

I gazed around, the posters swimming in front of my eyes. I'd seen *Hamilton* with my parents. It had been amazing, just like Leigh said. But what had made it more amazing was that it had been a rare time that our whole family had done something together. On the drive home, Dad had pulled up the soundtrack on his phone and we'd all sang along to some of the songs. Not well, but it hadn't mattered. Dad put on a French accent to do Lafayette, and Mom couldn't stop laughing. And neither of my parents had argued or complained, and for a short time after, I hoped that maybe everything between them would be better. But no.

They'd gone back to their yelling a few days later.

I pulled out my math textbook and started my homework. A few minutes later, Leigh came back to drop off my order, but as she set it on the table, she burst into a song about sugar and butter and flour. I assumed it was from a musical. She had a nice voice, but it was still kind of strange to be serenaded.

The cheesy fries were spectacular. They were amazingly crisp on the outside and fluffy on the inside. The cheese wasn't the fake kind, and it was generously sprinkled on top. And the shake! I'd never had roasted strawberry anything before, but it popped with berry flavors. By the time I finished both, I had done all my homework. Well, all except for the personal essay.

By then, the mommy club had left, but two other booths were occupied. I wondered what musicals were on the plaques on those tables. All I knew was that the one I was in was perfect for me. *Hamilton*. It was like a sign or something. Like maybe my dad was somehow with me here, even though he lived in Texas now.

I thought of the *Hamilton* T-shirt I'd stolen from him last year. Keiko's mom had just dropped me off. When I walked into the house, there were cardboard boxes stacked in the living room. I'd found Dad in the bedroom packing his clothes into a box.

"What's going on?" I asked.

Dad looked up at me, startled. "Jenna! You were supposed to be sleeping over at Keiko's."

I leaned against the doorway, clutching my overnight bag. "I wasn't feeling well."

Dad stood up and in two steps was at my side, hand on my forehead. "No fever. What hurts?"

My heart. But I didn't say that out loud. "My stomach. Maybe I ate too much."

Dad put his arm around me and walked me to the kitchen, where we always had a Japanese electric hot water pot plugged in. He sat me at the table and went to the fridge to take out a plastic container of sliced lemons. Then he grabbed a mug, squeezed a wedge of lemon into it, and pressed the button on the electric pot to release hot water into the mug. He slid it over to me and sat down.

"So," he said as I took a careful sip. "I'm moving out."

I clenched the mug, willing the tears not to fall. I cried only when I was alone, in my room, while listening to my parents yell at each other. I wasn't about to start doing it in front of anyone now. "I figured."

And that was all that had been said on the matter. Dad was gone two nights later, but not before I broke into one of the boxes and stole his *Hamilton* T-shirt. I already had one with the Schuyler sisters on it, but I'd wanted Dad's. It had been his favorite.

The first time Mom saw me wearing it, I could tell she wanted to say something, but she'd clamped her mouth tight.

I was startled out of my memory as Leigh broke into another song. This one I recognized from *The Lion King*. She carried a club sandwich to a man working on his laptop. He didn't pause as Leigh set the plate next to him but flashed her a quick smile.

I glanced at the time on my phone. I had better get going if I wanted to make it home before dark. As I packed up my books, Leigh came to take my dirty dishes. She handed me my bill and I paid her with my allowance.

"What did you think?" Leigh lifted the empty shake glass.

"It was delicious," I said.

Leigh grinned. "I hope you come back, Jenna. You're welcome anytime."

"Thanks."

I hitched my bag over my shoulder. As I got out of the booth, I ran a finger across the small *Hamilton* plaque. When I stepped outside, I glanced back into the smudged window. Nobody knew me here. I could be alone. I wouldn't have to talk about my feelings or run into Elliot. And that booth would be like Dad was with me.

I think I found my new perfect getaway.

five

The rest of the week, I kept my head down and avoided any interaction with Elliot. I also avoided writing my personal essay. But I didn't ask Ms. Fontes for a new assignment. Knowing Elliot was working on a sports article made me stubborn. If he could write about sports, then I could write a personal essay, no matter how useless writing one was. I knew I had to get to it, but the entire weekend sped by without me touching it.

After every newspaper club meeting, I went to the diner, making myself at home in the *Hamilton* booth. I could spread out. Nobody knew me, except for Leigh, who was friendly but didn't intrude. I got used to her singing when she served customers and realized that was why no music played at the diner. Fortunately, the diner wasn't that busy, so it wasn't constant and she only sang a few lines, not the entire song. The daily milkshake specials changed, but my favorite *Waitress* shake was always available. And I figured out that the sugar-butter-flour song went with it. Maybe I'd download the soundtrack.

By Tuesday, I was mildly panicked about my newspaper club assignment. The last thing I wanted to do was talk about feelings in a personal essay. How did that make for an interesting or important article at all? But I needed to at least bang out a draft. And I needed time to revise before handing it in on Thursday.

"Do not even!" Keiko nearly growled at me when I met her at her locker after school.

"What?" I asked.

"You're going to bail," she said, closing her locker with more force that usual.

Keiko didn't get angry often, and even when she did, she didn't usually show it. The fact that it was obvious was not a good sign.

I shook my head. "I'm not."

She relaxed her shoulders and gave me a sheepish smile. "Oh. Sorry."

I let her apologize even though she'd been right. I had totally come here to bail so I could work on the stupid essay, but I didn't want Keiko to be mad at me.

We fell into step as we walked to the gates leading off campus. When the wind kicked up, we both zipped our jackets and I tugged my hood over my head.

"What do you want to do on Thursday?" Keiko asked.

We'd ended up hanging out at her house last Thursday, walking her dog, Yuki, and watching TV.

"Whatever you want," I said.

"We should come up with something special."

It occurred to me that since seventh grade started, we never really fell into a routine together. Last semester, I hung out with Elliot most of the time. Before then, it had always been me, Keiko, and Audrey doing whatever Audrey wanted to do. Not that I missed Audrey and all her drama, but I did miss having a routine and a place to belong. Nothing felt normal anymore.

"We could watch a movie," I suggested. Keiko loved retro movies.

"It's okay," she said. "I've been getting my fix on Friday nights with the guys."

I'd forgotten that she went to Doug's to watch movies with them every week.

"We could study," Keiko said.

I laughed. Keiko was always trying to do things to make other people happy. "You don't want to study," I said. "Besides, we barely have any of the same classes."

I didn't remember it being so hard to come up with something to do together.

"I have a new chocolate cookbook," Keiko said.

"Does it have a cupcake recipe?"

"Definitely! There's one you would like. It's a banana cupcake with chocolate frosting."

"Let's make that one!"

Keiko's phone buzzed, and she pulled it out, squinting at the screen. She glanced at me and smiled guiltily.

"It's okay, Keiko," I said, meaning it. "You can text your boyfriend."

I expected her to blush or at least smile, but she looked serious.

"Keiko," I said, pulling off my hood. "I'm teasing."

She glanced at her phone again and tucked it back into her pocket.

My reporter senses tingled. Something wasn't right. "What's going on?"

"Um, I guess you can go do something else, if you want." Keiko wouldn't look at me. She sped up slightly, like she was trying to get rid of me.

"I said I wasn't going to bail. I'm here." I caught up to her. When did she get so fast? "I'm fine with watching the game. I'm happy about you and Conner." Did she think I was jealous or something? Or that seeing her with Conner made me all sad about Elliot?

I'd been impatient and short with Keiko since school started back up. I didn't mean to be like that, especially when I knew she only asked how I was feeling because she cared. But we'd been friends forever and she should know me better.

My chest tightened. Maybe from trying to keep up with Keiko. Maybe from something else. "Keiko, slow down. Don't be mad at me."

That stopped her. She swung around to me. "Oh, Jenna! I'm not mad at you!"

"No? Then why are you trying to get rid of me? You're

the one who made a big deal about me not bailing on you!"

Keiko hooked her thumbs under her backpack straps. "I'm not trying to get rid of you. I'm trying to be a good friend. I shouldn't force you to come to the game."

"You're not forcing me." I narrowed my eyes, and Keiko fidgeted. "What are you not telling me?"

Keiko sighed. "Conner texted."

"Okay."

"Elliot is there. Today's the three-on-three tournament. I guess he's covering it."

My bag slipped off my shoulder, and I just barely caught the strap before it hit the ground.

"Conner told me he's been interviewing the guys and he's staying for the game."

"Great." Elliot dumps me, and yet here he was showing up where I was. I didn't want to see him or talk to him, and I definitely didn't want to think about him anymore. I wanted him out of my head.

"Jenna, it's okay. I mean, you can come if you want, but you don't have to. I want to hang out with you, but it's not fair to make you be around"—Keiko paused—"him."

She was right. I didn't want to see Elliot. I especially

didn't want to see him working on his assignment when I hadn't even started mine. I didn't want his to be better than mine. I needed to get started on it.

"Thanks," I said. "I think I'll actually go work on my newspaper club assignment."

I walked to Leigh's Stage Diner, my thoughts swirling. Why couldn't Elliot stay clear of me? He'd acted like he cared about me when obviously he hadn't. If only he hadn't emailed me at the end of summer about the honors language arts reading list. If only I hadn't spent weeks alone at my dad's in Texas while he was at work, bored out of my mind while Keiko and Audrey were doing all the usual summer things without me.

Elliot had come along at the right moment, and I'd been weak. Our emails had turned into texts and even the occasional phone call. We'd talked about books and writing and newspapers. He was cute and smart, and I thought he liked me. But I'd been wrong. I hated being wrong.

I walked faster, clenching my fists. I thought about how Dad had left me and Mom. Opening yourself up to someone only led to pain. I'd never make myself that vulnerable again.

By the time I reached the diner, I was breathing hard, steam puffing from my lips into the cold air. I pushed the door open with a little too much force, making the bell jangle.

Leigh was busy ringing up a customer. I made a beeline to my table and then stopped short.

Someone was sitting in my booth.

six

I stormed up to the table, where a boy close to my age sat hunched over a notebook.

"You're in my booth," I growled.

The guy looked at me, surprise on his face. Then he looked pointedly at the tabletop. "I don't see a reserved sign." His voice was flat, a little arrogant.

That's when I recognized him. He'd been in my health class for a short time at the beginning of sixth grade. We'd been paired as study partners. He'd hardly cracked the textbook during in-class assignments. I'd had to badger him to do the work. He'd been snarky, calling me a teacher's pet. Thankfully, he transferred out two weeks later.

I'd kept my opinion of him to myself back then, but now, as I took in his black-rimmed hipster glasses and dark, carefully mussed hair that was obviously styled that way, he still looked every bit the slacker I'd pegged him to be.

"Rin Watanabe," I said. The tips of my ears heated. I totally hadn't meant to say his name out loud.

He smirked. "Jenna Sakai."

He remembered my name? I'd seen him around campus during passing periods over the last year, but we hadn't talked since he left honors health class. It had probably been too hard for him. That reminded me of the few times Elliot and I had been assigned to work on an article together. Elliot had a tendency to take over, even though I was perfectly capable of doing my share. I hadn't done that to Rin. Rin had just outright refused to do the work.

"There are plenty of other booths," I said.

"There are." He closed the notebook in front of him. It looked like a sketchbook.

"You can sit anywhere else."

"So can you."

Gah! What was his problem? I looked to Leigh for

help, but she was taking an order. There was no way I'd tell Rin why this booth mattered to me. Not that it would change his mind anyway.

Fine. I tossed my messenger bag onto the bench and scooted into the booth.

"Oh, sure," he said. "Come join me."

"I will. Thanks." I matched his sarcastic tone. If he didn't want to share the booth, he could move. I hoped he did!

He pushed his empty shake glass to the edge of the table, but he didn't leave. I took out my newspaper club notebook and rummaged through my bag for my pen case.

"Inuyasha," Rin said, almost under his breath.

I grabbed the zippered pen case covered with enamel pins and smacked it next to my notebook. "What?" Was he going to try to make conversation? I would have to end that right away. We may be sharing the booth, but that did not make us friends.

Rin nodded at my notebook covered with stickers. "Inuyasha. You read Rumiko Takahashi manga?"

Oh. Right. The manga I found at the library last year. I'd been impressed that the creator was a woman.

"I only read the first ten books," I said. There had been way too many in the series to keep up with and still do well in my classes. Something had to go. Manga reading was it. But sometimes I missed it. I'd gotten the Inuyasha sticker to remind me to pick it back up this summer.

It was typical that a guy fixated on the one sticker I had of a guy. Well, a half boy, half demon. The rest of my stickers were of powerful women like RBG, Michelle Obama, and sayings like SMASH THE PATRIARCHY.

"You should check out her horror series Mermaid Saga," Rin said. "It sounds sweet, but it's pretty terrifying."

Enough with the chitchat. "Look, I need to get some work done," I said, opening my notebook.

He shrugged. "Fine by me. You're the one who sat in my booth."

"Your booth? I've been here for the last week and haven't seen you. This is *my* booth."

"I had some other things to do last week," Rin said, "but I've been sitting in this booth since September."

I glared at Rin, and he glared right back.

"I'm glad to see you two know each other," Leigh said,

waltzing up to the booth. "I was wondering what would happen when you both showed up."

She looked way too amused.

"We're not friends," I said.

Leigh raised her eyebrows, and a small wave of shame washed over me. I cleared my throat. "We both go to Pacific Vista Middle School."

"The usual?" she asked me.

My eyes flit to the board, where Lulu's Strawberry Dream Pie shake held steady. The other shake of the day was the Sven Special.

Being a reporter, I couldn't let that go without inquiring. "What's the other flavor?"

Leigh nodded to Rin's empty glass. "An homage to *Frozen*. Vanilla slushy."

Hmm. Not very adventurous. I wasn't surprised. Rin probably didn't like new things or being challenged, which explained why he couldn't change booths.

"I'll take the *Waitress* shake, thanks."

I dug out my colored pens and lined them up above my notebook. I caught Rin watching and shot him a glare. He shrugged, opened his sketchbook, and picked up his black pen.

This time he caught me looking, which I guess he didn't like. So he grabbed the textbooks from his fancy backpack and made a wall in front of his sketchbook. Whatever! Like I cared what he was doing! I just had a curious nature, which was important for a reporter.

I picked up a green pen and twirled it as I thought about my assignment. I had skimmed one of those Modern Love essays Isabella recommended. It was about a woman who'd been dumped by her fiancé while visiting New York and then had gotten on the wrong subway on her way to Coney Island. She wrote about how she'd cried on the platform and how taking the wrong train was a metaphor for how lost she felt in life, blah, blah, blah. There was no way I would ever write anything so personal and, really, inconsequential. I needed to write *something*, though. I thought of Elliot and his three-on-three league article, and as much as I hated to admit it, it was an original angle. I already knew he was an excellent writer. Ms. Fontes would be impressed.

I scowled. I needed to do as well as, if not better, than Elliot.

Leigh's clear voice sang out, "Sugar, butter, flour," as she deposited my shake on the table in front of me.

When she was done, Rin started clapping. Leigh bowed before returning to the counter.

I raised my eyebrows at him.

He shrugged. "Every performer deserves applause."

Interesting. It was the first time I'd seen anyone clap for Leigh. I hated to admit it, but Rin was right. Leigh was talented, and she did deserve recognition. I wondered what song she had sung when she'd delivered Rin's shake. "Let It Go"? That would be impressive.

I took a sip of my shake and glanced at Rin, who was bent over his sketchbook. His pen moved in smooth strokes. What was he drawing? He must have felt me looking because he jerked his head up. I quickly averted my eyes to stare around the diner so he wouldn't think I was snooping.

The diner! Maybe I could write about it. That was personal. And this diner was unlike any I'd ever been to, that was for sure! I could write about how I found this place, describe it in great detail, talk about Leigh. I could ask her some questions about how she came to own and run this place. Yes! That would totally make an interesting article.

I started scribbling in my notebook. The words came quickly, and before I knew it, I filled two pages. Satisfied I had made a good start, I leaned back. The seat across from me was empty. But Rin's things were still there. I was dying to know what he was working on. A good investigative reporter didn't let opportunity pass.

I craned my neck to try to peer over the wall of books. I half stood and leaned forward, walking my hands across the table. When I touched something wet, my hand slipped, and I fell forward right into the wall of books, knocking half of them to the floor.

Gah! I got out of the booth and dropped to my knees, snatching up the books and hoping to get them back in place before Rin returned.

"Can I help you?" Rin's voice came from behind me.

I stood up, books clutched against my chest as I tried to come up with an excuse. Unfortunately, I was lousy at fiction. I was more about truth.

"These fell," I said.

I stacked the books on the table. That's when I noticed that Rin's sketchbook was closed. I wouldn't have been able to see anything after all.

As Rin sat down and set up his wall again, I grabbed

my notebook and pen and walked over to the counter, where Leigh was wiping down menus.

"Everything okay, honey?" Leigh asked as I sat on a stool across from her.

"Yes." I opened my notebook. "I'm writing an article and wanted to know if I could ask you a few questions about your diner."

She smiled widely. "An article about the diner? That's fantastic! It would be nice to get a little more traffic."

Leigh looked so happy, I felt horrible telling her that it wasn't for an actual paper. I wished I could just drop it, but I was all about the truth. "Actually, it's an assignment. It's not going to get printed or anything. Sorry."

To her credit, her smile didn't falter. "No need to apologize, Jenna. I'm happy to help you." She put the menus down and gave me her full attention.

"When did you buy this diner?" I asked, starting with an easy question.

"It was my dad's. I pretty much grew up here. He got sick with cancer and died seven years ago, and I couldn't walk away from this place. My husband, Tom, and I took over. No regrets!"

Oh. Not such a softball question after all. "I'm sorry

about your dad," I said. How horrible for Leigh. I missed my dad, but at least he was only in Texas and I got to see him on holidays.

Leigh nodded. "Thanks." She waved to the board. "Actually, he's the reason for the ice cream and the shakes."

"Your dad liked shakes?"

"When he was getting chemo, he lost his appetite. The one thing that he could and would eat was ice cream. I started making my own ice cream and then turning it into shakes. He really loved that."

"Wow," I said. "Your shakes are truly outstanding."

"Thanks."

"And why the Broadway theme?"

Leigh laughed. "Oh, how my dad is probably turning in his grave! The Broadway details are all me. This used to be a regular diner when it was my dad's. I wanted to be a stage actress. Broadway was the dream, but"—Leigh waved her hand to the diner—"this was more important. Carrying on my dad's legacy. And this way, I get to insert my own passion."

"That's brilliant," I said with a grin.

A family entered the diner, and Leigh went to greet

them. I walked back to my booth just as Rin was packing up.

"Later, Sakai," Rin said as he headed for the door.

I didn't respond. The only way Rin Watanabe would be seeing me later was from across the room. The *Hamilton* booth was mine, and I wasn't giving it up without a fight. I'd get here extra early tomorrow. He'd just have to find someone else to annoy.

seven

When I walked into newspaper club after school, Ms. Fontes smiled at me. "Jenna! How is your essay coming along? I'm so looking forward to reading it. Elliot just turned in his article."

Gah! He turned in his article a full day early. Of course. I joined Isabella at our table. She was wearing a Maya Angelou T-shirt. Last semester, Isabella had written an opinion piece about how poetry like Angelou's "Phenomenal Woman" and lyrics by Lauryn Hill changed the way girls saw themselves. I loved it.

"Hey," she said. "Thanks for your help with my article."

"Did you ever find out who the anonymous donor was?"

Isabella shook her head. "No, but I did find out exactly how much the donation was. A million dollars!"

I gasped. "That's a lot of cash!"

"Right? I focused the article on what that money could have paid for to make more important improvements. Updating the library, getting new computers, funding the girls' volleyball team uniforms."

"Or allowing us to put out a real paper. What a waste of money!"

"If I can have your attention for a brief moment," Ms. Fontes interrupted.

We all got quiet and looked up at her.

"I have some exciting news," she said. "The *Orange Country News* is sponsoring a journalism scholarship competition for college money. It's open to all middle and high schools in Orange County."

Most everyone started talking at once, shouting questions and whispering to one another. Elliot shushed the room, and everyone grew silent.

"Each school will get to submit one entry, and the winner from each school will get a fifty-dollar cash prize." Ms. Fontes smiled. "The grand prize is two thousand dollars for a middle school student and five thousand for a high school student to be put toward college, funded by the paper and a few generous donors."

I perked up. A cash prize and money for college! I needed all the help I could get. I'd overheard Mom complain on the phone to Auntie Kelley more than once about how Dad wasn't helping with college and how expensive it would be. And Mom had started harping on me about the importance of getting good grades so I could apply for scholarships. Not that I wasn't already getting straight As.

Elliot and I locked eyes. He would be my only real competition. I had to beat him.

"If you would all settle down, I can tell you the rest." Ms. Fontes laughed.

The room quieted once more.

"Assistant Principal Kim and I will be the ones selecting PV Middle's winning student entry. All students are eligible to enter with articles of their choosing, not just newspaper club members." Ms. Fontes waved her hand to keep us from protesting. "The applications are due to me on March fifteenth. After the winner is chosen, the entry will move on to the *Orange County News*. They will choose the winners in May. Perhaps you'd like to consider this most recent assignment as your entry. Whatever you decide, I can help you hone and polish over the next few weeks. I'll email you the application and details. Now get to work! Your assignments are due tomorrow."

I would not be submitting a fluffy personal essay. There was no way I could win with that. I glanced again at Elliot, who, of course, was looking my way, a small smirk tugging at the corners of his lips. I didn't need to talk to him to know he was thinking the same about his sports piece. We would both be working on something else for sure. I just had to make sure my story was better. I needed a hard-hitting investigative piece.

I knew who would probably get to enter from PV High. Olivia Rose was the editor of the high school's paper, the *Big Wave*. She used to babysit me, Keiko, and Keiko's little sister, Macy, back when I was in the third grade. Olivia lived around the block from me, and I saw her once in a while. I read her articles all the time since the *Big Wave* was online. I couldn't wait to get to high school and write for the paper.

"Are you going to enter the competition?" Isabella asked me.

"Definitely! You?"

Isabella shook her head. "Probably not. I mean, I don't want to work on this assignment anymore. I want to get back to writing what I love, music and fashion."

"You could enter with one of those. Your Maya Angelou piece," I suggested, pointing to her shirt.

"Yeah, but I don't really have time to work on it. My sister wants me to sew some of the designs we created over break. She thinks she can sell my skirts!" Isabella smiled. "Anyway, you know it's going to come down to you and Elliot."

She was probably right. Not that she wasn't good enough if she wanted it, but the truth was, Elliot and I were the ones to beat. We just cared more than anyone else. And I needed to win.

I spent the rest of newspaper club so focused on trying to come up with ideas for an article that would be worth entering that I'd forgotten about beating Rin to the diner. When I got there, he was already in my booth.

I stalked over, refused to greet him, and sat down. Today Rin had on big headphones, and he'd already set up the wall of books around his workspace. I wondered what kind of music he listened to. He was hard to read. He wore a Hurley hoodie, which was not cheap, and his glasses looked designer. His dark hair was sleek, almost blue black. Probably the same color as mine would be if I stopped coloring it. Which I wasn't planning on doing anytime soon.

Leigh walked up to the table. "Jenna, it's good to see you. What will you have? Sorry, I ran out of the strawberry ice cream."

I glanced at Rin's side of the table. He was still working on a shake. It looked like some sort of chocolate concoction.

"It's the Chocolate Shake Where It Happens," Leigh said. "Our double chocolate ice cream with hot fudge."

A *Hamilton* shake! "That might be too much chocolate for me," I said even though I loved the connection to the musical.

"I just made a triple berry lavender ice cream last night. You want to try that in a shake? I'm calling it Dear Berry Hansen."

"That sounds good," I said.

"And Fetch Fries with Cheese?"

I shook my head. "Not today." I couldn't afford to have a shake and fries three times a week. Well, I could with the guilt money Dad had given me for Christmas, but I put that into my college fund. As usual since the divorce, Dad went over the top with gifts. He'd not only thrown money at me but also bought me a new iPhone. I guess to match the new laptop he'd gotten me over summer.

Leigh left with my order, and I pulled out my essay to make some notes. It wasn't bad. After I turned it in, I could focus on coming up with the perfect article for my scholarship application.

"I'm tapping on the glass, waving through a window," Leigh sang as she dropped off a very purple shake. I clapped for her. Rin caught my eye, and his lips twitched in an almost smile.

I took a sip and closed my eyes. I didn't know what she did to her ice cream, but it was seriously the best.

"You have a thing against chocolate?" Rin asked me.

"What are you talking about?"

"You told Leigh that this"—he pointed to his mostly empty shake glass—"was too much."

I glared at him. "How did you hear me over your music?"

"Oh, I'm not listening to anything right now."

"That is deceiving!" I'd have to be careful around him. He was definitely sneaky.

"What are you working on?" he asked.

I folded my essay in half. "What are *you* working on?"

His face closed up.

"You started it," I said.

"You didn't answer."

"Neither did you."

For some reason, he broke into a grin. His whole face changed when he smiled. Gone was that slacker vibe, and instead he radiated warmth. Rin tugged his headphones down so that they draped over his shoulders. They were broad. I wouldn't be surprised if he worked out or something. I bet he was arrogant about his looks.

I glanced back up at his face, and his grin had stretched even wider.

"Shut up!" I snapped, feeling the tips of my ears grow hot.

He chuckled. "I didn't say anything."

"You have something on your shirt." That was better than admitting I was checking him out.

He glanced down and ran his hand along his chest. He had long, tapered fingers. "I don't see anything," he said.

"Hmm. You must have gotten it."

I went back to reading my essay and finishing my shake, and Rin went back to whatever he was doing behind his wall of books. But I couldn't concentrate. I might as well head home.

I gathered my things and shoved them into my messenger bag. If Rin thought I was being rude, I didn't care. I paid at the register and left.

I'd have to get here before him next time. I needed my booth back. But if he did get here before me again, then I would at least have to employ some sneaky tactics of my own to find out what he was working on. Because one thing was for sure, I was an excellent investigative reporter.

eight

"You're hanging out with Rin Watanabe?" Keiko asked as we walked into her kitchen on Thursday afternoon. She let Yuki out of her crate, and the fluffy dog pranced around our feet.

"'Hanging out' is a generous term," I said, leaning down to pat Yuki on the head.

Keiko already had the ingredients for banana cupcakes with chocolate frosting set out on the counter, but my sweet tooth was calling and it wouldn't wait. I dug in the pantry and found one box of chocolate-covered Pocky sticks and one of strawberry. We both liked the chocolate better. I held them up.

"Jan-ken-pon?" Keiko asked, smiling.

We'd used the Japanese chant for rock, paper, scissors to make fair decisions ever since we were kids. I put the boxes down, and we held out our fists.

"Jan, ken, pon!" we chanted, shaking our fists. On "pon," we flashed our choices. I spread my hand out in paper, and Keiko kept hers in a fist for rock.

"I win!" I chortled, wrapping my hand around her fist.

"Fine." Keiko reached for the strawberry Pocky, but I stopped her. I handed her the box of chocolate. She smiled. "You sure?"

"I'm sure." I opened my box and ripped open the foil bag inside.

Keiko handed me five of the chocolate-dipped cookie sticks. "So, Rin Watanabe, huh?"

Why had I spilled about the diner and Rin to Keiko? She was already getting ideas. I shook my stick at her. "He stole my booth. I refused to let him have it, so we're sharing it. It's not like we talk."

"Hmmm." Keiko crunched through two Pocky sticks.

She was about to say something annoying, I could just sense it. I counted backward in my head, *Five, four, three, two ...*

"He's kind of cute, isn't he?" Keiko asked.

"Don't," I said. "This is so not about that."

"I was just making an observation."

I raised my eyebrows at her. "Okay, then, objectively, yes, he's good-looking, in a shojo-manga-boy-hero way. Should I tell Conner he should worry?" I asked.

Keiko blushed. "Not even."

Wow. She really had it bad for Conner. Which was fine. For her.

"When can I go to the diner with you?" Keiko asked.

"Because you want to check Rin out?" I smiled, teasing her.

"Stop! No!" She laughed. "Fine! Keep the diner and Rin to yourself for now, but I definitely want one of those chocolate shakes soon. And I totally want to hear Leigh sing. What a cool place."

I nodded. "Right? I can't believe more people don't know about it. Not that I want it to get too popular."

After we finished our snack, I played sous chef to Keiko as she mixed the batter for our cupcakes.

"How's newspaper club going?" Keiko asked after she turned off the mixer.

"Fine. Ms. Fontes told us about a scholarship competition for college tuition."

"Really? That's awesome!"

"I need to come up with the best article ever. Only one student from PV Middle will get to enter." I'd turned in my personal essay after school, and I was glad to never have to look at that again. Now I could focus on whatever I would write for the contest.

"Maybe that will calm your mom down," Keiko said cautiously.

"Yeah. Maybe." I got quiet. A few months earlier, I'd let it slip to Keiko that Mom was getting all hyper about college already. Once I graduated from high school, Dad's child support obligation would end. I had overheard part of Mom's call with Auntie Kelley. I knew if I asked for details, Mom wouldn't give me a straight answer. More likely it would get her on a rant against my dad, and I didn't want to hear that. The only good thing that came from the divorce was that I didn't have to hear them shouting at each other anymore.

It wasn't as if we ever hurt for money. Dad made bank at his corporate job. I never understood why Mom had to always point out what the money she made as a CPA bought. I thought when couples were married they shared the money, but what did I know about that.

Keiko cleared her throat and then pulled the bowl from the mixing stand. "Any idea what you'll work on?"

I shook my head. "Not yet, but my article needs to be better than Elliot's."

Keiko grimaced.

"What?"

"You and Elliot."

"What about us?" I placed paper cups in the cupcake tin, making sure not to put the same two colors side by side.

"You were both always trying to outdo each other."

"True." Even though we hadn't had any of the same classes, Elliot and I constantly compared our grades. "But we studied well together. His competitiveness actually kept me sharp."

Keiko handed me a spoon, and I portioned the batter into the cups.

"I know one thing," Keiko said.

"What?" I set the timer as Keiko put the cupcakes into the oven.

"Whatever you write is going to be smart, interesting,

and totally deserving of that money. You are a Super Reporter!"

We high-fived. And then, like the best friend she always was, she let me lick the spoon.

~

On Friday, I walked into newspaper club late. It was the only way I could be sure that Isabella was already there to sit with and avoid any awkward encounters with Elliot. How weird that Elliot and I had spent all our free time together, every day at school, after school, and some Saturdays, talking and writing, and now, nothing. Like we had never existed.

"Good afternoon, reporters," Ms. Fontes said. "You all impressed me with your assignments."

I leaned forward, elbows on my desk. I couldn't wait to see what Ms. Fontes thought. I may have resisted the personal essay at first, but like any good reporter on deadline, I had delivered. I was pleased with the result.

"I've marked your papers with comments. I want to see revisions next week."

A groan went up around the room. We weren't done with this assignment? I was ready to move on.

"This is part of the process, kids. Revision. You know that."

"Will we get a new assignment after the revision?" I asked.

Ms. Fontes gave me a look I couldn't interpret. "I'm going to let you all pick your next assignment. That way if you want to work on something else for the scholarship, you'll have time." She nodded. "Okay, come get your papers and get to work. I'm here if you have questions or want to discuss my comments."

I jiggled my leg impatiently. I couldn't believe I wasn't done with the essay. I wanted to work on something important. I waited till everyone else got their papers and then made my way up to Ms. Fontes. The buzz in the room grew as people discussed the comments on their papers.

"Jenna." Ms. Fontes handed me my essay.

There were no comments or marks on it. My heart soared. Did she think it was perfect?

"This was a good attempt," she started, not sounding at all like she was about to tell me I was on my way to becoming a Pulitzer Prize-winning journalist.

I rolled the paper in my hand.

"But this was not a personal essay," she said. "This read more like a profile of the owner of the diner, and while it was interesting and well written, it wasn't the assignment."

The tops of my ears burned. I was glad for the noise in the room so that no one, especially Elliot, could hear what Ms. Fontes was saying.

"It *was* personal," I said softly. "I talked about how the diner makes me feel."

"Yes, I saw that you had a little of that. It barely skimmed the surface, though. I would have liked more about you, your thoughts, your feelings. Why do you like this diner? Why is it important to you?" Ms. Fontes raised her hand to stop me from doing what she said we shouldn't when we're getting feedback. Defending or making excuses. I clamped my lips tight. "Dig deeper, Jenna. There's a reason this diner is so important to you."

I sighed, not knowing what to say.

Ms. Fontes gave me an encouraging smile. "You are an excellent writer. You can do this, Jenna. I want a complete rewrite. I'll email you some examples that I think might help."

"Thanks." I tried to sound grateful. I forced a smile and kept it on my face as I returned to my seat.

"How'd you do?" Isabella asked. Before I could answer, she showed me her paper. "I only have to make a few tweaks. Ms. Fontes said I wrote a compelling piece!"

This time my smile was real. "I'm glad."

I opened my notebook and doodled, pretending to write. All I could think was that I had failed. I have never failed at anything in school. In fact, the lowest grade I ever received was a B-plus on a math test I'd taken when I had been coming down with the flu. I hated to perpetuate the stereotype of studious Asians, but I was proud of my good grades. And I needed the good grades to get college scholarships. Winning this journalism scholarship was really important. It would help me, and it would help Mom be less stressed.

I didn't need to look at Elliot's paper to know how he had done. He was crowing to Ben and Carlos and waving it around.

At least I wasn't getting a grade for this. Newspaper was just a club. It was supposed to be fun. Only I wasn't having fun.

Isabella nudged me. "I'm going to be so glad when

this revision is over. I heard about this cool coffee shop that has a youth open mic night once a month. I totally want to write about it."

"You're not going to work on the cafeteria donation article anymore?"

She shook her head. "No, why?"

My heart sped up, and I felt a tickle of anticipation run up my spine. "Can I have it?"

"What do you mean?"

"Can I write a follow-up?"

Isabella smiled. "Go for it!"

This was it! I was going to find out who that donor was, why they wanted to be anonymous, and why they didn't use the money to do something more important than make the cafeteria pretty.

I was going to write the best article ever and be PV Middle's entry for the Orange County Junior Journalism Scholarship!

nine

On Saturday, I went to my first Carter family game night in ages. Keiko hadn't been kidding. Mrs. Carter took Scrabble very seriously. The best part was how cowed Doug and Teddy were by her. Keiko and I giggled through most of the game. I teamed up with her and Teddy, and Doug teamed up with Mr. Carter and Keiko's little sister, Macy.

Mrs. Carter and Conner soundly trounced the rest of us, but Keiko's dad made up for it with banana key lime pie. When we were all stuffed and Scrabbled out, I got a ride home with Doug's mom and the guys.

"Tell Keiko to suggest a different game next Saturday," Doug said to me from the front seat.

"Yeah, any other game!" Teddy said.

Conner laughed.

"You don't get to laugh," Teddy said to Conner, punching him in the shoulder. "And next time we play Scrabble you can't team up with Mrs. Carter!"

Doug turned to me. "Conner always calls her first."

"Hey!" he said, grinning. "You just wish you could be as quick as me!"

"What other games do they have?" I asked. "Oh, maybe Yahtzee!"

"Yeah! That's the one with dice, right?" Doug asked. "Let's play that one next week!"

"You'll make it happen?" Teddy asked me.

"I'll do my best."

When I walked in the front door, I found Mom sitting in the living room reading a book. "How was game night?" she asked as I took off my shoes and placed them on the shoe rack by the door.

"Good," I said.

Mom smiled. "And the Carters?"

"Fine." Mr. Carter and my dad used to work at the same company, so our families used to hang out together a lot. That's how Keiko and I became friends even before I moved into her school district in the third grade. But when Dad and Mom started to have problems, they stopped seeing all their friends, at least together. My dad had stayed friends with Keiko's dad even though they didn't work together anymore. I think maybe Mom thought Keiko's parents took sides, and everything got awkward. I was glad that had never happened between me and Keiko.

"Too tired for a movie?" Mom asked.

"Never!" Mom rarely stayed up late. This was a bonus. "Popcorn?"

"Sounds good."

I followed Mom into the kitchen. "I can make it, you know. I am perfectly capable of using a microwave. In fact, since I'm turning thirteen next month, maybe I can even use the stove when you're not home?"

Mom grabbed a bag of microwave popcorn from the pantry. "We'll talk about it when the time comes."

Which probably meant no. "I'm not going to burn the house down, Mom."

"I'm less worried about the house and more concerned about your safety." Mom popped the bag into the microwave and pushed the popcorn button. I didn't tell her that Keiko and I were allowed to use the oven at her house.

The microwave hummed while I pulled out the popcorn bowl from the cabinet. The new one. Because Mom had tossed out the old one we used to use with Dad.

"Speaking of your upcoming birthday," Mom said as the popcorn started popping. "What do you want to do?"

Another thing that had gone out the window was our tradition of going out to the movies as a family on my birthday and then to my favorite sushi restaurant. Last year, Mom sent me to the theater with Keiko and Audrey. It had been fun, but it wasn't the same.

"Sushi?" I asked hopefully.

The microwave beeped, and Mom opened the door to grab the hot bag before I could.

"Maybe," she said, dumping the popcorn into the bowl.

I filled two glasses with water and led the way back to the living room. Mom sat down and set the popcorn bowl between us. She started the next movie on our queue. It was a mystery. Mom loved those.

Mom and Dad used to argue jokingly over the movies we watched. Dad liked comedies; Mom liked mysteries and thrillers. Before I was old enough to stay up with them, I used to overhear them bartering. Dad would offer to wash her car for a movie or Mom would offer to mow the lawn. At first they'd been teasing each other, but by the time I was ten, it had gotten much more heated. By then, though, they fought about everything. Movie choices, chores, money, and even stupid things like who left the lights on.

Halfway through the movie, the main characters—a married couple who was trying to solve a murder—started to argue about their finances. I think it was to make us realize that the murder happened because of money, but it made me want to run and hide in my room. It felt way too familiar.

Mom paused the movie. "Bathroom break," she said.

While she went down the hall, I refilled our water glasses. I wished I could fast-forward through this scene.

Mom sat back down and picked up the remote. "You know, the wife should totally get a job. That way she wouldn't be reliant on her husband."

"Hmm," I said. Mom rarely talked about things, so I was careful not to say or do anything to stop her.

"It's important for you to get a good job, Jenna. That's why I want you to go to a good college. If you have a great career and make your own money, you won't ever have to rely on a partner. Remember, money is power, and power is independence."

"Did Dad not share the money he made?" I asked.

She glanced at me, embarrassed for being so transparent. She shook her head. "That's not the point. The point is your dad made a lot more money. And he never let me forget that."

"Like how?"

"We'd better get back to the movie. It's getting late." Mom hit the remote and the movie started back up, but I couldn't focus on it anymore.

I remembered hearing Mom tell Mrs. Carter that she'd grown up with parents who were very traditional. Grandma had been a stay-at-home mom while Grandpa had worked. Mom had made a comment about how sad a life Grandma had had, but anytime we visited my grandparents, they seemed happy and loving. Maybe it had been different while Mom was growing up. I wished Mom would tell me stuff.

"That was exciting," Mom said.

The movie was over. I had no clue who the murderer was. I rubbed my eyes.

"Go to bed," Mom said gently. "Do you want to drive up to LA tomorrow? We can go to Little Tokyo, hit the Japanese American National Museum, and then go shopping."

"That would be fun," I said.

I got ready for bed, but I couldn't fall asleep. I missed Dad. Why did Mom have to be so obsessed with money? I remembered one particularly loud fight about the stove. It had broken, and Mom had blamed Dad because he had picked it out. She insisted on buying the next one with her money. Dad had said all their money was her money. In the end, though, he'd chosen the stove. Again.

But maybe Mom was right. If I could earn enough scholarship money and somehow pay for college on my own, I wouldn't have to rely on either of my parents. Then she could stop being mad at Dad, and Dad could stop throwing money and gifts at me. He probably only did that to make Mom angrier. This Orange County Junior Journalism Scholarship could be the start of my financial independence. I liked how adult that sounded.

That meant I had to write a good personal essay and get it out of the way so I could focus on the scholarship entry. Then I could figure out who that ridiculously rich donor was and why they'd earmarked the money for the cafeteria. And why remain anonymous? That seemed suspicious to me for sure. I shifted in bed restlessly, my curiosity refusing to be quieted. And then I realized something. I didn't have to wait. I could work on both stories at the same time.

I closed my eyes to try to get some sleep, but when I did, all I saw was Elliot's smug face when he'd gotten his assignment back from Ms. Fontes.

He thought he'd win the scholarship. He didn't think that I was good enough.

I couldn't believe I'd ever liked him.

ten

I loved Mondays. It was a fresh start to the school week. I always had all my homework completed and was prepared for any tests. Today I was in an especially good mood. Saturday with Mom had been awesome. And Dad had sent me an email with a link to an article about Japanese American journalists. I was inspired!

I was also distracted, so I forgot about my plan to get to newspaper club late and instead walked into the room early to find only Elliot there. I ignored him and went straight to my new table. Elliot followed me.

"What are you doing?" I said, sitting down hard in my chair.

He raised his hands. "Hey, you don't have to be so—"

I cut him off. "Do not even say angry."

Elliot looked sad. "Jenna, I don't want to be like this."

"Well, maybe you should have thought about that before you got all superior and arrogant."

"That's not what happened, and you know it."

I shook my head. "That is what happened, but you choose to pretend it away."

"See? That's what I was talking about. You're not objective."

"I'm not talking to you about this anymore." I turned my back on him and dug through my messenger bag for my notebook and pen case.

"I only came over here to see how you're doing on the scholarship application."

"Why? So you can steal my idea?"

"Oh my God, Jenna!"

I unzipped my case and started pulling out my pens. "Just leave me alone."

Elliot turned to leave but first said, "Fair warning. I have a great lead on an article. I'm going to be picked for PV Middle's entry."

I gripped one of the pens so hard, it dug into my palm

sharply. When I looked down, I realized it was the pen I'd kept from Elliot. I slammed it back into my bag and grabbed my own blue pen.

"You okay?" Isabella sat down next to me.

"Yep."

She peered at my face. "You don't look okay."

Why were people so obsessed with talking about things that didn't matter? "I'm fine."

"Mmm-hmm. Right."

I was relieved when Ms. Fontes strolled into the room with the rest of the club members.

Today she had us practice writing headlines. We'd done this in the fall, but it had been challenging for most of us. Ms. Fontes handed out short articles, and we had to write headlines for each. It took half an hour, and then she let us work on final revisions. Well, everyone else worked on final revisions. I was supposed to be rewriting my personal essay.

I watched Elliot walk over to his usual computer. He sat in the chair and, as always, scooted it forward a bit, then back, and then forward. I used to tease him about that. Carlos sat at my computer. Well, it wasn't mine, but it was the one I used whenever Elliot and I had worked side by side. I shook my head, like a dog shaking off muddy water, and approached Ms. Fontes, who was grading papers at her desk.

She looked up. "How's the essay coming along, Jenna?"

"About that," I said. "I was thinking I could get started on my article for the scholarship application."

Ms. Fontes smiled. "I think that's admirable. But what about the essay?"

I held in a groan. "It's not like we have to do the assignment, right? I mean, this is a club, not a class."

Ms. Fontes put her pen down. "Jenna, while it's true that we are a club and we aren't putting out an actual paper, every member is still expected to pull their own weight."

PV Middle didn't have an official journalism class or a school paper. Something about lack of funds. Which reminded me of the one million dollars that went to renovating a cafeteria that had been perfectly functional. Yeah, the food was much better now and the cafeteria itself was gorgeous, but who really cared? That money, or part of it, could have funded a school paper and gotten us new computers.

"I know," I said, "but it makes no sense for me to write this essay."

I think I surprised us both with my statement. Ms. Fontes blinked at me like I was a stranger. I kind of felt like one. When had I ever refused to do an assignment?

"Jenna, part of working on a newspaper is being a team player. Sometimes an editor might assign you something that isn't exciting or fun for you, but if you want to work your way up the ranks, you're going to have to put in your time. I think this personal essay is a good challenge for you. I look forward to seeing what you write."

Ms. Fontes picked up her pen and went back to grading papers. I returned to my seat, opened my notebook, and doodled, stewing.

"Those are pretty good," Caitlin said, peering over my shoulder at my notebook.

"These? They're just doodles. Scribbles."

Caitlin pointed. "That's a bowl of ramen. A burrito. And mochi. I love mochi!"

"Yeah. I do, too." I studied my drawings. Each food item was like a cartoon character with big anime eyes and mouths. Like I said, silly doodles.

"You want to draw a comic strip with me?" Caitlin asked.

"What? No!"

Caitlin looked offended.

"You're a real artist. I just doodle. You're seriously talented."

Her face relaxed. "Okay, well, if you change your mind, let me know." She wandered back to her table.

I doodled other foods for the next twenty minutes. I drew a chocolate bar, a sushi roll, a pizza slice, and a bubble tea character.

"What are you working on?" Isabella returned from using a computer and sat next to me. "Oh, those are cute."

I sighed. What a waste of time! I should have been working on my article.

"Okay, spill it, Jenna," Isabella said. "You seem upset. And don't tell me you're fine when it's obvious you're not."

I huffed out a breath. "It's just that Ms. Fontes insists I write this personal essay. I want to focus on the article I'm writing for the scholarship."

"Do both!"

"I could, but the more I think about it, the more I don't want to bother with the essay." I glanced over at Ms. Fontes, making sure she couldn't hear me. She was talking to Ben. I leaned closer to Isabella. "Ms. Fontes may be a great language arts teacher, and she's super chill for sponsoring this club, but she's wrong to make us work on things that have nothing to do with real journalism. Plus, I really need this scholarship."

Isabella nodded. "I get it. So, write the article. It's not like she can kick you out of the club for not working on the essay."

Isabella had a point. I gathered my things. I was not looking forward to the next club meeting. The shine of newspaper club was wearing off.

eleven

Dad always said Sakais weren't quitters. In third grade, that had kept me working on my multiplication tables when I got frustrated. In fourth grade, it had kept me on the soccer team. I was good, but I didn't love it. And now I supposed it should make me want to stick it out with my essay.

I mean, it was a good motto. The reason journalists like Christiane Amanpour, Lisa Ling, and Gwen Ifill were successful was at least partly because they never gave up. But Dad hadn't followed the family motto when it counted. When his marriage was in trouble, he quit.

So I didn't feel that bad when I skipped newspaper club on Wednesday. Besides, I wasn't really quitting. I was just taking a break. Like Isabella said, Ms. Fontes couldn't kick me out of a club, at least not while I maintained the required GPA. I could use the time to work on my scholarship application entry.

I headed straight to the diner. The thought of getting there before Rin and reclaiming my booth made me speed-walk with anticipation. I was slightly out of breath when I pushed the door open triumphantly.

That feeling lasted all of two seconds. Rin was already in the booth. How had he gotten here so quickly?

"You thought you were going to beat me here," Rin said as he tugged his headphones down so that they hung around his neck.

I refused to answer him.

"Jenna, you're here early," Leigh said. "I made more roasted strawberry ice cream for you. The *Waitress* shake is back on the board."

I smiled. "Thank you!"

"Or you can try the Berrily We Roll Along shake. It's blueberry basil."

Rin pointed to his teal milkshake. "We could call it

the Jenna Special since it matches her hair," he said with a smirk.

"Well, then you could name a shake after Rin," I countered. "Call it the Grumpy Bear shake."

Rin's eyes widened. "You think I'm grumpy?"

Leigh chuckled. "Hmm, maybe I *will* name shakes after you two. You're my most loyal shake customers. Fetch Fries, too?"

"Not today," I said.

"I'll take an extra-large order," Rin said.

When Leigh walked away, I scowled.

"What?" He frowned. There. That looked more like the Rin I knew and loathed. "I'll share with you."

"I don't need charity."

"Who said it was charity?"

"I don't want your fries." Mom's comment about money and power echoed in my head. No way was I giving Rin any power over me.

"Fine. Don't have any."

"I won't!"

Rin put his headphones back over his ears and returned to drawing in his sketchbook behind the wall of books.

Leigh sang a song from *Mean Girls* as she dropped off our orders, which made me crabbier. Why should she sing the song for Rin's order and not mine? He undoubtedly already got a song with his shake.

But when I sipped my shake, my mood evened out. As always, it was delicious. It felt good to have something familiar and comforting. Like this *Hamilton* booth would be if Rin would just leave it.

I eyed Rin's fries. He had already made a dent in them while continuing to draw. The smell of fried potatoes made my stomach rumble, but I wasn't going to have any. Not after I'd made such a big deal about it.

Anyway, what was up with that wall of his? This reporter needed to know what he was doing back there. I prided myself on following through on my curiosity, on getting the story, on finding the facts. The truth.

The next time Rin looked up, I held his gaze and moved my hand to his wall of books. I hovered my hand over his science textbook in the middle. He leaned back in his seat and crossed his arms. Was he daring me? Or giving me permission?

I touched the book with my fingers. No reaction from Rin. I grabbed it and laid it flat, getting a view of his sketchbook. I craned my neck to get a better look. Rin sighed as if he were annoyed, but he spun the sketchbook around to face me.

"Manga?" I asked, studying a black ink drawing of a guy in a spacesuit-like uniform wielding a baton that seemed to be a weapon of some sort. Sparks flew from the tip. Or maybe it was a fat wand. It was an excellent drawing.

"You drew this?" I wanted to immediately smack myself. Of course he drew it. What kind of reporter asked a question with an obvious answer? "I mean, it's really good."

"Thanks."

"Are you taking art classes? Do you know Caitlin Shimizu?"

He shook his head and looked annoyed.

I rolled my eyes. "I'm not doing that thing where I assume all Asian people know each other. I asked because she's in the art program."

"I know that." He still looked annoyed, his mouth in a frown and his brows creased. "I'm not in the program. But I know who Caitlin is."

Okay. *Come on, Jenna, just be cool and get the info.* I

needed to practice my investigative journalist skills as often as possible.

"Do you draw every day? Just for fun, then?"

"Pretty much." Rin spun the sketchbook back his way.

"Can I see some more?"

He held up the book—careful to keep it out of my reach—and flipped through a couple of pages. His drawings were amazing! Good enough to be in a graphic novel. But by the third page, I noticed something and made an involuntary sound.

"What?" Rin slammed the book shut.

"Hey! I wasn't done."

"You made a noise!" Rin shoved his sketchbook into his backpack and with a scowl imitated my earlier response. "Tsk, tsk."

Wow. Sensitive. "I really like your drawings," I began. "They're really expressive..."

"But?"

"But I noticed there aren't any girl characters."

Rin stared at me for a long moment and then burst out laughing. The sound tickled my ears and trilled down my spine. It almost sounded like music.

What was his problem? It was my turn to scowl.

I waited for Rin to stop laughing. It didn't take long.

"What's so funny?" I asked.

He shook his head. "I thought you were going to say something else."

"Like?"

Rin's face closed down again. I liked it better when he smiled and laughed. He actually had a nice laugh.

"Come on," I said. "I'm curious."

He shrugged. Rin did that a lot. "Fine," he said. "I thought you were going to say something about manga not being real art."

"Why would I say that?" I snapped. I hated when people made assumptions about me.

Rin finished off the rest of the fries. It didn't look like he was going to answer. I needed to change my strategy. A good reporter was able to get a subject to feel comfortable enough to reveal things.

I chased the snark out of my voice and tried again. "Seriously. Why would you think I would say something so judgy? You already know I like manga."

He played with his napkin, folding it and unfolding it three times. His hands were smooth, and his fingernails were trimmed neat and short. "It's what the sixth-grade art teacher said to me the first week of school."

"That's horrible! What kind of teacher says something so rude to a student? A good teacher encourages!" For a brief moment, I thought of Ms. Fontes, but I shut that down quickly. "And it's probably racist. I mean, just because it's a Japanese cartoon style doesn't make it inferior! Would the teacher have said the same thing if you'd been drawing characters that looked like the Scarlet Witch or Wonder Woman?"

Rin shrugged. "No clue. I switched electives."

"But—" I started.

Rin waved. "Yeah, I hear you about the female characters."

"And?"

He shrugged again. His cheeks looked a little pink.

Okay, time to push gently. I had to know. "There's a reason you draw only guy characters?"

He nudged the empty plate away from him. "I started drawing when I was six or seven."

"Okay." I made my voice encouraging. Friendly.

Rin started unfolding and folding his napkin again. His fingers moved quickly and smoothly. I waited him out. I could be very patient when it mattered.

"They were me," he finally said so quietly I had to lean forward to hear him.

"Oh."

"Well, not anymore they aren't," he said, his voice defensive as he crumpled the napkin in his hand. "Kids play make-believe, okay? Instead of pretending to fly like a superhero or turn my sister into a frog, I drew it."

"Hmm. Clever," I said.

"I'm not really trying to live out my fantasies that way anymore. I draw, but for fun. But I guess that's why I never thought about drawing a female character—not because I have anything against girls. Women," he quickly corrected. When I gave him a look, he said, "I have an older sister. She'd like the stickers you have on that one notebook you write in all the time. What's it for anyway?"

It felt wrong to tell him to MYOB after all my prying. "It's for my newspaper club assignments."

"Cool." He nodded and then returned to drawing in his sketchbook, ending the conversation.

Irritation prickled me. I'd listened to him talk about his art, but he didn't have anything to ask about my writing? Rude.

But then I remembered something. Rin and I weren't friends. It didn't matter what he thought. And anyway, he'd taken my critiques a lot better than most people would.

I glanced over at him, totally lost in his sketchbook. Only this time, he hadn't put the wall of books back up.

twelve

"Dude, what three things would you want to have in a zombie apocalypse?" Doug asked me at lunch the next day. He caught my scowl and coughed. "I mean Jenna. Jenna, what three things would you make sure to have?"

Teddy and Conner laughed at him.

"Shut up," Doug said, smiling.

At least he was trying to stop calling me dude. "Hmm." I pondered. "A long sharp sword, flint, and my bike."

"Why not a car?" Teddy asked.

"You think gasoline will be easy to get?" Conner interrupted.

Keiko shook her head. "I'd be the first one turned. I have no survival skills."

"We'd protect you," Conner said.

They smiled at each other and held hands. I had to admit, just to myself, that they were adorable.

As Doug and Teddy continued planning for the zombie apocalypse and Conner and Keiko whispered to each other, I glanced up and saw a familiar black backpack attached to a familiar form wearing familiar headphones. My eyes followed Rin all the way across the field. I wondered where he spent lunch. In fact, I could practice my investigative skills and tail him.

"I have to get something from my locker," I said, standing.

"I'll go with you," Keiko said.

"No, it's okay," I said quickly. "I'll see you after school."

I took off down the bleachers before Keiko had a chance to tag along. I trotted across the field, keeping my eyes on Rin, and followed him into the main building and up the stairs as closely as I dared.

But when I peered around the corner, he was gone. Gah! I walked down the hall, peeking into empty classrooms. Then, suddenly, I heard instruments tuning up in the music room. Students sometimes had lunch in the band room like our newspaper club members hung out in Ms. Fontes's room. I wondered who Elliot was eating with now. Probably Carlos and Thea. I felt a pang of regret. Not over Elliot, but just over having a place to be.

Since I'd lost Rin, I decided to peek into the music room before heading to my locker. I stopped in the doorway and looked around. Half-eaten lunches were strewn on empty chairs, and a small group of students sat in a semicircle practicing a song. I was about to step back into the hall when I noticed Rin unpacking a guitar.

I ducked out of the room before he could see me and nearly ran back down the hall, my heart hammering. But then I stopped myself. Why was I running? He hadn't seen me. I had every right to be there. I went to this school! I smiled. Knowing where Rin spent lunch and that he played the guitar made me feel powerful. Like I knew a secret.

There were only a few minutes left of lunch, and I had to grab my science homework. When I got to my locker, Keiko was there.

"Hey, I thought you said you had to get something

from your locker." Keiko leaned against the lockers, arms crossed.

"How long have you been waiting here?"

"A while! I was only a few minutes behind you."

"I had to do something for newspaper club first," I said. It wasn't a complete lie. I mean, tailing Rin was practice for life as a reporter. I spun the combination to my locker. "Why'd you follow me anyway?" I asked, a bit too harshly.

Keiko's eyes went wide, and then she started blinking quickly. I was getting way too good at hurting her feelings.

"You don't have to push me away, Jenna. You made your point. I won't ask you anything about Elliot, okay?"

I exchanged my books as the silence between us drew out. I took a deep breath. When I closed my locker, I forced a smile. "What do you want to do today after school?" I asked her. "More baking?"

"Actually, that's why I was looking for you. I forgot that I already have plans today."

"Oh?" I deserved this. Of course, she didn't want to hang out with me anymore. I'd been snapping at her a lot.

"Yeah. Conner got us tickets to a special showing of *Spirited Away*. It's this evening, so we're going to do our homework and then have dinner. I meant to tell you earlier."

"It's fine." I waved my hand. Miyazaki films used to be our thing. I hadn't even known there was a special showing. "I have to work on my scholarship article anyway."

"See you on Saturday at game night, though, right?"

"It's okay. I don't need to come. It's probably more fun hanging with the guys."

"What are you talking about? I want you there!"

"Okay. If you're sure."

"I'm sure, Jenna."

The bell rang. Keiko tucked a lock of hair behind her ear, gave me a long look, and headed off to her pre-algebra class. The stiffness in our friendship tugged on me for the rest of the day and didn't loosen up, even when I saw Keiko at PE. We didn't talk—Coach Yang had figured out we were best friends and kept putting us on different teams to keep us from gabbing. We weren't even on the same volleyball court. And I felt somehow relieved. Keiko would still be hurt, and I'd only feel guilty. Better to just give us some space.

After PE, I was the first person out of the girls' locker room and ran—RAN!—to the diner. When I got there, I slammed into the front door, shoving it open...and gasped.

"Do you skip last period or something?" I panted as I walked over to Rin, who was already sitting in my booth.

Rin shot a too-happy grin at me, like he'd won a race. But he didn't have his headphones on yet, and he was still unzipping his backpack, so I couldn't have been too far behind him.

I threw myself down on the bench just as Leigh brought two glasses of ice water over. "I thought you two could use these, the way you come charging in here."

"Aha!" I shouted, pointing at Rin. He had the decency to look busted at least. But the grin stayed on his face.

Leigh smiled. "Shakes today? The usual?"

"Yes, please," I said after taking a big gulp of water.

Rin glanced at the specials board. "That *Hamilton* chocolate shake for me."

"You got it," Leigh said. "Fries?"

"Yeah, large," Rin said. He gave me a look. "To share."

I didn't fight Rin on that. I'd pay for my half. I was starving after all that exercising in PE and then running here.

"Okay, time to fess up," I said after Leigh walked away. "You've been trying to get here before me."

He raised his hands. "Guilty." Then he flashed that annoying grin again. "And I've been winning!"

"Whatever," I said. "That isn't fair. I didn't know it was a race."

"Hmm, competitive much?" Rin pulled out a textbook, but instead of putting it up to build a wall, he opened it.

I gasped loudly, clutching my chest. "Is that an actual schoolbook you're opening?"

"You're hilarious, Sakai," Rin said.

Leigh sang a few lines from "The Room Where It Happens" and dropped off our shakes and a platter piled higher than usual with cheesy Fetch Fries.

After Rin and I applauded, he nodded at the notebook on my side of the table. "Newspaper club stuff?"

"Yep."

"What are you working on?"

I grabbed a fork and stabbed some of the fries. I blew on them, then shoveled them into my mouth to stall. I didn't want to have this conversation with Rin. My life was none of his business.

"Well?" Rin asked, pulling the platter toward him.

I reached out and stabbed another forkful. I thought about Keiko and how she was angry with me. I wished I could discuss this with her instead. I wanted to talk to someone about it. Rin was here. He was convenient. "I'm investigating the cafeteria renovation."

"That sounds boring. Who cares about that?"

"I do!" I gripped my notebook. "Someone anonymously donated a ton of money to update the cafeteria. Why? And why spend that kind of cash on the cafeteria when there are other more important things that need upgrading."

"Wait, someone gave money to redo the cafeteria?"

"Right? It's stupid! Our computers are old and glitchy. Our library is dark and dingy. Obviously, the donor has too much money and doesn't know what to do with it. Rich people are ridiculous!"

"What? You lost me . . ."

"It's like the more money they have, the less conscious they are. The donation could have gone to fund extracurriculars." Funding a school paper would have been nice. "Anyway, it's going to be fun writing an exposé."

"Wow, Sakai, you are the ultimate nerd."

I drank the rest of my shake, giving myself brain freeze. "If you think that's insulting, it's not." I rubbed my temples with my fingers. "'Nerd' is just another word for 'smart.'"

Rin shrugged. "Fine. Whatever. How are you going to solve this mystery?"

I couldn't tell if he was making fun or asking a serious question. "I have skills," I said vaguely.

"Hmm. Okay, what do we do first? Break into the school records?"

"First off, there is no 'we.' And second, I won't be breaking any laws." Isabella hadn't had any luck with the office staff, but there were other ways to get the info I wanted.

"Aw, come on. Let me help."

"I don't need your help. I work on my own." I learned that lesson from Elliot. Every time we'd worked together, he took over, like he thought his ideas were better. The first article we'd cowritten, he took home and edited without my input. He'd taken out most of my stuff. Another time, I'd given him an idea, but then he'd told Ms. Fontes he came up with it, taking all the credit. When I'd brought it up to him, we'd gotten in a huge argument.

Working on my own was the smarter way to go.

I opened my notebook. Thankfully, Rin took the hint and began to study. It was very strange not to see him drawing. I flipped my pen between my fingers, pondering next steps. I mentally ran through the list of the staff at school and came up with a brilliant idea—I could talk to Mr. Kim! The vice principal would probably know the name of the donor. Plus, since he was on the judging committee for the journalism scholarship, it wouldn't hurt to show him my dedication.

I heard Rin grumble to himself. When I glanced up, he was spinning his pen, too, and glaring miserably at his textbook.

"What are you studying?" I asked.

Rin stopped spinning his pen. "Plant biology."

"Awesome! I love science!"

He gave me a look. "Of course you do."

I rolled my eyes, grabbed his worksheet, and slid it over. He didn't stop me. I read the first question out loud. "What is the purpose of a flower?"

"It's useless information." Rin started twirling his pen again, spinning it so fast between his fingers that it was a blur.

My pen spinning had annoyed Elliot. I think it mostly

bugged him because he couldn't do it. I had joked that there was an Asian gene for pen twirling. That had annoyed him even more.

"Why are you frowning like that?" Rin interrupted the memory.

"It's not useless information. It's science!"

"You can keep saying that, but it doesn't make it more interesting. I'll never need it anyway."

"How can you know that? Do you already have your career path set?" I pushed the worksheet back at him and reached for his science book.

"Pretty much. And flowers won't be a part of it."

That was weird. And why did he sound so glum about it? I flipped through the textbook. "Here!" I stabbed a finger at the page. "Here's the answer." I spun the book back toward him.

He pushed his glasses up with his finger and glanced at the book. "I know how to read."

"I didn't say you didn't. I'm just trying to help you." I didn't mention how useless he'd been in health class. He probably didn't remember anyway.

"You may be a teacher's pet, but I don't need your help." Or maybe he did remember.

Rin took the worksheet back from me and filled in the answer. I moved my bag and scooted next to him so I could see his paper. As I peered at it, my shoulder touched his arm. It was solid and muscled and warm. I flinched away like I'd had an electric shock.

"You think this is fun, don't you?" he asked as he continued writing.

"What are you talking about?" My voice squeaked. I could still feel the warmth from his arm on my skin.

He gave me a quick look. "Homework? You think homework is fun."

"Oh yeah. Right. Yes," I babbled. I moved back to the safety of my side of the booth and observed from afar. He wrote quickly and smoothly. Almost the same as when he was drawing.

Twenty minutes later, he was done, and from what I could see, he'd gotten all of them right, without looking at his textbook. I was speechless.

"God, that was torture," Rin said when he finished. He shoved his textbook back into his backpack. "You should learn how to have fun, Sakai. Relax."

He'd known all the answers! Maybe he wasn't as incompetent as I thought. "Learning is fun," I said.

"Okay, then, what do *you* do for fun? Besides draw."

He shrugged. "I play the guitar, but you knew that."

My ears flamed and burned a trail across my face. "What?"

"I saw you at lunch in the doorway to the band room."

"Oh. Um, I . . ." Words wouldn't come to me. I cursed my brain. Writing was always easier than speaking. "I have to get going."

"I'll pay."

"No, you won't. I can pay for my own food."

Rin got up, but I was faster. I had no doubt his family was like my own Japanese family and fought over the check at gatherings with friends and family at restaurants. Not polite motions, but full-on scene-making squabbling, grabbing, and yelling for the check.

And I'd learned from the best. My mom was the champion. I made it to the register first, smacked down enough for my half of the bill, and left before Rin had a chance to catch up.

I tried to let triumph over winning that small victory fill me, but since he was still in my booth, it felt like Rin had won instead.

thirteen

I marched into PV Middle's main office first thing the next morning.

"Jenna Sakai, what a pleasure to see you." Mrs. Bauer, the school clerk, smiled at me. I had helped out in the office once a week after school in sixth grade for community service credit.

I smiled. "Hi! Is Mr. Kim in?"

"Let me check."

Mrs. Bauer came back after a couple of minutes. "You're in luck. He's free. Go on in."

"Good morning, Jenna," Mr. Kim said when I entered his office.

I set my notebook and pen on my lap as I took a seat across from his desk. "Hi! Thanks for seeing me."

"Is everything okay?" he asked.

"Yes. I'm working on an article for the Orange County Junior Journalism Scholarship application. And I had some questions for you."

"I think Ms. Fontes would probably know more details about the application process, but I can try to answer your questions."

"Oh, no, not about the application, about my article. I'm writing about the cafeteria renovation."

Mr. Kim smiled. "Ah yes! That was such a wonderful project!"

Wonderful? Not likely. I opened my notebook. "Why do you say it was a wonderful project?"

"Well, the kitchen equipment was old. The oven was broken, and we'd repaired the freezer at least three times in the last year and a half. But then we had a generous benefactor swoop in to save the day, so to speak."

"I heard that the donation was a million dollars," I said.

Mr. Kim looked surprised. "You are quite the investigative reporter, Miss Sakai."

"Thank you." Actually, thanks to Isabella for making that discovery and sharing it with me. "Who was the donor?"

He shook his head. "I'm not at liberty to say."

Hmm. A little obstacle won't deter me! "Well, that was a lot of money." I jotted a note to research how much it really cost to renovate a cafeteria. "Did it come with conditions? Or could it have been used for other projects, say, after-school clubs for example?"

Mr. Kim leaned back in his chair. "I'm not sure what direction you're heading in with this article, but let me assure you that this donation was not only generous but necessary."

I didn't like his tone. He was treating me like some kid when I was a serious reporter! I needed him to just spill the info already.

"Why does the donor want to remain anonymous?"

"I can't answer that. Perhaps they didn't want attention for their generosity." Mr. Kim glanced at the clock on the wall. "The bell will be ringing soon. You need to get to first period."

I packed up my notebook and stood. "Thanks for your help," I lied. I needed to stay on his good side.

He'd be judging my finished story after all.

Mr. Kim smiled. "Good luck with the article. I'm glad someone is going to write about the project."

If that were true, he'd give me the information I needed. I hoped I could dig up something earth-shattering to make my article stand out. Then my tenacity would impress him and Ms. Fontes, too. I just needed that donor's name!

~

That afternoon, I didn't bother changing out of my gym clothes before rushing out of PE. It was Friday, and I had to take them home to wash anyway. I pulled sweatpants over my shorts and threw on my jacket. And I ran out of there.

Gah! Somehow Rin still beat me to the diner!

"How do you do it?" I gasped, throwing myself into my seat. I peeled off my jacket. I was all sweaty. "You're not even out of breath."

He smiled but didn't answer.

Leigh's clear voice sang the sugar-butter-flour lines and stopped at our table. "One *Hamilton* chocolate shake and one *Waitress* shake."

"I didn't order yet," I said. "But thanks."

Leigh nodded at Rin. "He ordered for you."

The smile dropped off my face. "How do you know I didn't want the *Hamilton* shake?" I said to Rin.

"It's chocolate," Rin said. "You said it was too much chocolate for you."

"Back then! Maybe today I feel like too much chocolate."

Rin rolled his eyes. "Fine, then take the chocolate one."

Leigh gave me the chocolate shake, then picked up the roasted strawberry.

"Where are you going with that?" I asked.

"I'll make another chocolate one," Leigh said.

"Oh, I'll take it." I reached out for the strawberry shake and nudged the chocolate one to Rin.

"You won't have to pay for that, Jenna," Leigh said. "Rin paid the whole bill last time, so you have a credit."

I glared at Rin. "Then I'll pay the bill today."

"You two are exhausting," Leigh said, laughing.

Rin shrugged and grinned. He took out his sketchbook but didn't put up his wall of textbooks.

"Done with all your homework?" I asked.

"I don't need another mother, thanks."

I smirked as I took out my notebook. I only had math homework today and already finished it during class. Keiko and I were going to study together on Sunday. I was relieved to have some time alone with her. I promised myself I'd be super nice.

The sound of Rin's pen moving across paper made a soothing soundtrack as I brainstormed other ways to find out who'd paid for the cafeteria.

"How goes your investigation?" Rin asked, reading my mind.

"Fine."

"Did you find out who donated the money?"

"I'm not sharing information with you." My phone buzzed with a text. Mom was picking up Thai food for dinner.

"Who's that?" Rin asked.

"Wow, you're nosy!"

"See? I'd make an excellent partner to help solve your mystery. I could totally break into the school office and look through their files."

"Like I said, I don't need help, especially from a delinquent."

Rin didn't look at all offended. "Okay, so what's your plan, then? Hacking the school computer system?"

"You're a hacker?"

"No. Why? Would you let me help if I were? I could find one."

"No!" Gah! He was so annoying!

He shrugged, then deliberately and slowly put his wall of books back up around his sketchbook. He was such a child! I didn't care if I couldn't see what he was doing. In fact, I'd had my snack and done as much work as I could on my article. There was zero reason for me to stick around.

I slipped out of the booth, paid Leigh for Rin's order to even the score, and went home.

When I got there, the house was empty. As I set the table, my phone buzzed and I assumed it was Mom telling me she was on her way, but it was Dad. I'd texted him a few times this week, and he hadn't answered. Even if he was busy, he usually sent a quick emoji to let me know he'd seen my message. Only I hadn't heard from him all week. As I sat down on the couch, I wondered what his excuse would be. Too tired? Busy with meetings? Going out to fancy restaurants?

Hey kiddo! Sorry I haven't been in touch. I was traveling.

Just got off the plane now.

That was a new one. Dad didn't travel much for work.

Where were you?

Japan.

I sat up so quickly my phone shot out of my hands. I caught it in midair, and forgetting I was mad at Dad for ignoring me, my thumbs flew over my screen.

WHAT?! No way! I want to go to Japan!

How long were you there? Where did you go? What did you eat?

My phone rang. "Hey, Dad."

"I can't keep up with you on text. I can't type that fast." Dad laughed.

My anger disappeared. It was nice to hear him laugh. We'd laughed a lot over Christmas break. Unlike summer, when I'd spent most of it alone in his tiny apartment with ugly rental furniture, Dad had taken the whole week off from work. We'd gone ice-skating and mini-golfing, and he took me to this cool printing museum. It had been a good Christmas even though it was sad and weird not being with Mom, too. She had flown to Oregon to spend it with Auntie Kelley.

"Dad! Japan!" I prompted.

Dad told me all about his business trip. He'd gone to Tokyo for a week. I was so jealous!

"I promise to take you one of these days," Dad said. "I got you a few things. I'll send them your way soon."

"Awesome! Thanks, Dad!"

The garage door rumbled open.

"Hey, Dad? I have to go."

"Ah, your mom is home." Dad's voice got quiet. "Okay. Talk later, kid."

I dropped my phone onto the coffee table just as Mom walked in the back door.

"Dinner has arrived," Mom announced as she took off her shoes. "Whew. What a long day. I'm exhausted."

"Movie?" I asked hopefully.

"Sorry, Jenna. I had to bring some work home. Why don't you call Keiko?"

I took the bag of Thai food from Mom and walked it to the kitchen. "It's okay. I have some homework. I'll see her tomorrow at game night."

Besides, I'd brought work home, too. I was going to do some more digging. There had to be someone I knew who could get me the information I needed for my article.

fourteen

A week later, I hadn't had any luck figuring out how to find out the donor's identity. It was beyond frustrating.

"Is that chocolate fudge?" Teddy asked.

Keiko brought out a little plastic container from her lunch bag. She smiled as she passed it around to the guys. She turned to me. "I made you something else."

"You did?"

Keiko handed me a cupcake. "I tweaked that banana cupcake recipe. It's now banana strawberry with cream cheese frosting."

I took a big bite. "Yummy," I said, wiping frosting from my mouth.

Teddy nudged my leg with his foot. Ah yes. "So, for game night tomorrow, can we play Yahtzee?"

It was my second attempt. Last Saturday was Scrabble yet again. At least that time I'd teamed up with Mrs. Carter for the win.

"Sure," Keiko said, laughing. "We'll have to play something besides Scrabble anyway."

"Why's that?"

"Macy hid it."

"Your sister rocks!" Doug shouted, punching the air.

"How's your mom doing?" Keiko asked when I'd finished the cupcake.

"Fine."

Keiko waited for me to say more, and when I didn't, she sighed quietly. I felt like all I did was disappoint or hurt her these days.

"Do you want to come over for dinner before game night starts on Saturday?" she asked.

I kind of wanted to wait to see if Mom would be around for dinner, but I didn't want to risk alienating Keiko even more. She was the only friend I had left. "Sure."

Keiko smiled, and that made me happy. Now if I could

only make headway on this article for the scholarship! Time was ticking.

~

After school, I lurked in the hall that connected to Ms. Fontes's room. I saw Isabella and waved her over.

"There you are!" Isabella said. "What happened to you?"

"I got busy," I said.

"With?"

I shook my head. "Actually, I wanted to ask who you talked to when you were investigating the cafeteria donation."

"All the office staff," Isabella said. "Nobody knew. Mostly they were all excited about the donation. I got the feeling that to the school administration, at least, it was a great thing."

"Yeah, I got that impression, too." I sighed. "How are things going with you?"

"Good. Ms. Fontes gave me the go-ahead on my next article." Isabella glanced over her shoulder. "You coming in?"

"Not just yet." I didn't want to see Ms. Fontes until I had a better lead on my article.

Isabella turned and started walking to the classroom. "I hope you come back soon, Jenna. Club's not the same without you."

I nodded as I contemplated my next move. I needed a computer.

Elliot poked his head out of the room, and when he saw me, he smiled. I steeled myself as he approached, a bounce to his step.

"Hey!" Elliot said. "What's up? Why haven't you been around?"

That's why he was so chipper. Probably glad to lose some competition. I wanted to tell him not to get too comfortable, but I wasn't about to show my cards.

"What do you want?"

"Nothing. Just wondering what happened to you."

"That's none of your business." Not anymore.

"Why were you talking to Isabella?"

"Again. Not. Your. Business." I pushed past Elliot and made my way to the library. I could use a computer there. I knew I could go home to use my laptop, but I didn't like being alone in my empty house, waiting hours for Mom. The diner would have to wait. It was apparent that I would never beat Rin there, anyway. He was also getting sneakier about paying. I was going to have to have a talk with Leigh to make sure I paid my own bill. There was no way I would let Rin have any kind of power over me.

One of the computers was free. I hurried over before someone else took it, pulled out my newspaper club notebook, and opened a search engine. There had to be someone outside our school who knew about the donation.

"What are you doing?" Elliot's voice came from over my shoulder.

I swung around. "Why are you following me?" I said. The person using the computer across from me flashed me a dirty look. I lowered my voice. "Seriously, Elliot, don't stalk me."

"I'm not stalking. I'm curious. What are you working on?"

"Homework. Now stop being a creep and go away!"

I waited till Elliot left the library before turning back to my screen. I knew he was trying to find out what I was working on for the scholarship application. If we were still together, we'd probably be talking about our articles and sharing information.

We'd been inseparable, though, not one of those

disgusting, mushy couples who seem joined at the hip. Elliot and I just loved the same things. We talked about current events and watched documentaries. He was my go-to person. I loved Keiko and she was my number one best friend, but she didn't get my passion for writing. I mean, she totally listened to me go on and on, but with Elliot, I could have these amazing, intense conversations about the world beyond Pacific Vista.

But he'd lost the right to know anything about my life when we broke up. Suddenly, my mind was filled with memories of last semester.

Our first argument. We'd been talking about the *Big Wave*—the high school paper. Elliot had said Olivia Rose's pieces weren't as strong as David Wang's and that he should have been the editor. I totally disagreed. Elliot said I was biased because I knew her. That had nothing to do with it. But he didn't listen when I tried to tell him that.

The arguing got worse when Ms. Fontes assigned us to work on articles together.

Elliot insisted on putting his name first on the bylines.

"It's alphabetical," he said. "Both ways. E before J. O before S."

"Yours was first for the first article we did," I said. "And this one was my idea, so I think my name should be first."

Elliot grimaced. "Not like we need to specify whose idea it was, but this one was mine."

"It was not!"

Elliot shook his head like I was a toddler throwing a tantrum. "Fine, you can put your name first. Geez, Jenna!"

"Because it was my idea," I pushed.

Elliot didn't respond. And I let it go, or so I'd thought.

During our last newspaper club meeting before Christmas break, Ms. Fontes had praised us both on the article. She called it an original idea.

We'd stayed after everyone else had gone home for the day to exchange gifts and hang out just the two of us before I had to leave for my dad's.

"You're very smiley," Elliot had said, taking my hand and squeezing.

"It was nice that Ms. Fontes thought my idea was original."

Elliot dropped my hand. "Your idea? It was mine."

I was in too good a mood to let him bother me. "It doesn't matter," I said. "I'm just glad Ms. Fontes liked it."

I turned to get Elliot's present out of my bag.

"What is your problem?" he asked.

"What do you mean?" I replied slowly, my defenses rising at the edge in his voice.

"You keep trying to claim credit!"

"Because I deserve credit!"

Elliot rolled his eyes. "Jenna, let's face it. You're smart. You're talented. But you're not going to get very far if you're always this competitive."

I coughed back a laugh. "Competitive? With you? Not even! You're the one stealing my ideas, my work!"

"Oh, Jenna," Elliot said in that condescending tone I was starting to really hate. Our voices were raised, and if anyone was out in the hall, they would definitely be able to hear us. Just like I'd heard every word my parents shouted at each other before the divorce.

"You think you're better than everyone else."

"Because I am!"

I couldn't believe he'd just said that.

"All we do is fight," Elliot said. "And obviously you don't respect me."

"*You* don't respect *me*!"

Neither of us said anything for a long while. Elliot

started packing his things up. "Maybe we shouldn't be together, then."

"You're right for once. Maybe we shouldn't be together!"

"Fine!" Elliot stood.

"You're leaving?" I asked.

"What else is there to say?"

I wrapped my arms around myself like a hug. "So, now what? We're broken up?"

Elliot was in the middle of turning toward the door, but he swung back toward me so fast he stumbled. "You're breaking up with me?"

"No, *you're* breaking up with *me*!"

"Oh, that's just great, Jenna! You have to compete over this, too?" Elliot shook his head and stormed out of the room.

I blinked myself back to the present. I was so much better off now that we'd broken up. Being alone wasn't so bad. It meant not fighting over stupid things. Not giving away power.

And not ever getting hurt.

fifteen

"There you are!"

I jumped as Isabella came up behind me at the computer. She sat down in the empty seat next to me. I glanced at the library clock, surprised that an hour had flown by while I was researching and lost in my memories.

"I'm glad I found you. I don't have your number, so I couldn't text you."

I smiled as we exchanged phone numbers.

"How's it going?" she asked, nodding at the computer screen.

"I keep hitting dead ends." In my research *and* my

relationships. "How about you? What's your new article about?"

"That's why I'm here," she said, grinning. "You busy this evening?"

"Why?"

"I'm going to that youth open mic night I was telling you about. I'm writing about it. Want to come along?"

Oh wow. Isabella and I had never hung out outside newspaper club. But Mom was working late. Keiko had her movie-night thing with the guys. I was tired of coming up empty for this article. Maybe my brain just needed a break.

"Sure. Sounds good."

"Cool! It's at Dune Street Roasting Company. It starts at five thirty. Do you need a ride?"

I nodded. Mom wouldn't be home in time for sure, and the coffee house was too far for me to walk, especially at night.

"We'll pick you up in an hour. Is that enough time?"

"More than enough. Thanks!"

I raced home to drop off my books, leave a note for my mom, and grab a hoodie, and before I knew it, Isabella's mom was pulling up outside. When I climbed into the back seat of the Prius, Isabella turned and grinned at me. Her mother reached her hand between the seats.

"It's a pleasure to meet you, Jenna," she said. She wore blue-and-yellow beaded earrings that swung as we shook hands. Her warm smile was identical to Isabella's.

"Thank you for the ride, Mrs. Baker," I said, fastening my seat belt.

"You're welcome. I love meeting Isabella's friends."

Mrs. Baker started driving and we talked about our favorite songs. It turned out Mrs. Baker and Isabella loved *Hamilton*, too. She turned on "My Shot," and we sang together. And for the first time in a long time, listening to the soundtrack made me happy instead of just making me miss my dad.

By the time she dropped us off at the coffee shop, there was already a line out the door.

"Is this usual?" I asked.

"No idea," Isabella said. "But it has to be a good sign, right?"

We got in line behind a group of giggly girls our age. I didn't recognize them, but our school was huge.

"Your mom is fun," I said.

"Thanks. I like her." Isabella laughed.

"So, how does this work? What kind of acts are there?" I asked, nodding to the coffee shop.

"Any kid who wants to can sign up. Singers, poets, any kind of performance. I heard that last time three stand-up comics in a row totally bombed."

Ugh. That sounded painful. I hoped this would be at least semi-entertaining. But it was definitely better than sitting at home alone.

"Hey, Jenna Sakai!" I spotted Olivia waving from near the front of the line.

I grinned and waved back.

"Who's that?" Isabella asked.

"Olivia Rose, the editor of the *Big Wave* at PV High."

"Isn't she a senior?"

I nodded. "She used to be my babysitter back when I was in the third grade."

"Nice connection, Jenna! Go talk to her!" Isabella nudged me.

"Now?"

"I'll hold our places."

As I made my way up to the front, the middle school girls complained.

"I'm not cutting," I snapped. "I'm just saying hi to a friend."

"Hey, Jenna, long time no see!" Olivia was wearing a cute floral-print miniskirt with a black T-shirt. "This is my girlfriend, Marina."

"Hi," Marina said. Her long brown hair was pulled up in a high ponytail.

"Hi, Marina," I said, smiling.

"How have you been?" Olivia asked.

"Good. I'm in the newspaper club."

"Excellent!"

"I've been reading your articles for the *Big Wave*. They're really great."

"Oh, another groupie," Marina said, teasing Olivia.

"Ha-ha," Olivia said. She turned back to me. "Are you applying for the scholarship?"

I nodded. "You?"

"Sure am. I'm working on an article about the oil spill last month."

"Wow! That's going to be intense and awesome," I said. I was surprised Olivia was so willing to share. Not that I would steal it. It was nice that she was so trusting, at least with me. It made me feel safe with her. "I'm trying to work on finding out who made an anonymous donation for our cafeteria renovation."

"PV Middle got a new cafeteria?" Olivia asked.

"Yeah! It's totally fancy, like a food court, all upgraded. I want to find out the donor's name and why they funded the cafeteria when they could have funded more important things."

Olivia nodded. "That is going to be an outstanding article."

"Yeah, but I'm stuck. I can't figure out who the donor is."

"Don't give up," Olivia said as the doors to the coffee shop opened.

"Thanks!" I made my way back to Isabella.

"Good chat?" she asked when I rejoined her.

I nodded. I wanted to be as good a writer as Olivia when I got to high school, and I totally wanted to be editor of the *Big Wave*. She had been the first junior to be made editor, and the first one to be editor for two years. I wanted to be the next. That meant working hard at my craft.

By the time we got into the coffee shop, the place was packed with no open tables. There were chairs along the back and the sides of the shop. Isabella hurried toward two chairs, but they were snagged before we got there.

"Jenna!"

Olivia stood and pointed to two empty spots at her table.

"Score!" Isabella said. "We're right in front of the stage."

Score was right. I didn't care about being close to the stage, but I did care about spending more time with Olivia.

As Isabella got out her notebook and pen, I made introductions.

"Also in newspaper club?" Olivia asked.

Isabella nodded.

"Isabella writes amazing articles about music and fashion," I said.

Marina pouted. "I'm the only nonwriter here."

"Aww, I still love you," Olivia said. She turned to me. "Marina's cousin is performing tonight. He's a beat poet."

The lights dimmed, and the crowd quieted. A lanky man with a goatee stepped onto the makeshift stage, which was really just part of the coffeehouse floor marked off with blue tape and a microphone.

"Welcome to the third youth open mic night! I see word is getting out. This is our biggest crowd yet! I'm Avi, the manager of Dune Street Roasting Company. All coffee drinks are buy one get one half off."

A few people got up to buy drinks.

"We have a pretty full lineup today, so let's get started. Our first act is the Lindstrom sisters."

A cheery song started to play over the speakers, and two teenagers leapt out onto the stage and started singing. They were pretty good. After that was Marina's cousin, who was spectacular. He got a ton of applause. Then someone Olivia and Marina knew did a decent stand-up routine, followed by two mediocre high school bands.

The lights brightened, and Avi came back onstage to announce a short intermission.

I leaned over to Isabella. "You think anyone from our school will perform?"

"I hope so."

"What's your article's focus?"

Isabella tapped her pencil on the table. "I'm planning to write about youth open mic, but I'd love to feature one of the performances from our school."

"Fingers crossed, then," I said.

We smiled at each other.

"Hey, Jenna, I just thought of something," Olivia said.

"What?"

"My aunt is the superintendent of our school district."

"Cool."

Olivia waited a beat, a small smile playing on her face. The tips of my ears burned as realization struck. "Oh! Yeah?" I asked. "Do you think she'd tell you?"

"I think so."

"But would you be able to tell me after?" I wasn't sure how that worked.

"As long as she doesn't say 'off the record,' we're good!"

"Isn't that kind of sneaky, though?" Marina asked.

Olivia shrugged. "Got to get the facts to get the story," she said, winking at me. "Give me your number, and I'll text you if I find out anything."

When the lights dimmed again, I sat back, feeling full of hope and happiness. This was the best night ever! Not only was I hanging out with Isabella, but I got to spend the evening with Olivia, and she might be able to get what I needed for my article. And maybe she'd even write me a letter of recommendation for the high school paper or something. If that was even a thing.

Isabella got her wish. The next act was a group of kids from our school's drama club. They did a dramatic reading from last fall's performance of *Little Women*. Isabella and I exchanged looks. They were good, but nothing to write home about.

Three more acts later, Avi announced the last performance.

"Those of you who have been to youth open mic night before will be happy to see our most popular act from last month return."

A burst of squeals came from the back. I spun in my chair and glared at the cluster of middle school girls I'd seen outside blushing furiously. Yeesh. At least it looked like this might be what Isabella needed for her article.

"Let's welcome back Rin Watanabe!"

Cheers came from the back again as my brain froze. "Wait, what did he just say?" I asked out loud as Rin stepped out onto the stage, an acoustic guitar strapped to his back, where I was used to seeing a black backpack.

Rin walked to the center of the stage and sat on a high stool. His black hair neatly swooped across his forehead instead of his usual tousled look. He wore a plain charcoal-gray T-shirt and dark jeans. My heart sped up. I shrank back in my chair like it would make me invisible. I didn't want him to see me.

Rin adjusted his guitar and strummed a chord. Another girl squealed quietly and was hushed by her giggling friends. Gah! This was ridiculous. It wasn't as if Rin were some rock star.

Then the world melted away as Rin started to sing. His voice was rich and melodious, reminding me a bit of his laughter. I stared at his hands as he strummed. I didn't recognize the song, but it was folksy and smooth. He sang about lies and secrets and how they could shatter a heart. I could relate. The way Mom and Dad tried to keep me in the dark, the surprise of the divorce and Dad moving away, and how neither of them ever told me anything. Lies and secrets could shatter the heart if you let it. Good thing I was stronger than that.

Rin transitioned into the bridge, doing some fancy finger work, and sang a line about forgiveness. If I were the swooning type, which I definitely was not, I could see getting swept away. I guess I could give those giggling girls a break.

As his song wound to an end, I was relieved. Soon I would fade into the crowd and escape. I risked a glance at Rin's face as he strummed the last chord, and our eyes met. My breath hitched, like I was on a roller coaster. He gave me a small smile, and Isabella's head whipped to me so fast I felt air waft in front of my face.

"You know him?"

Rin stood, and the room burst into applause. The lights went up, and a gaggle of girls quickly swarmed him.

I said a quick goodbye to Olivia and Marina, and grabbed Isabella's arm, hustling her out the door.

"Yeah, I know him," I said finally. "But not as well as I thought I did."

sixteen

Monday after school, armed with questions Isabella wanted me to ask Rin, I walked into Leigh's Stage Diner. As expected, Rin was already in my booth, wall of textbooks up and headphones on. I stopped at the counter.

"Hello, Jenna," Leigh said. "How are you?"

"Good. Can you please let me pay for my own food?"

Leigh smiled. "Aww, why not let Rin treat you? He seems to really want to."

Only because he wanted to prove he was better than me. I didn't want to be beholden to Rin for anything. "I'd rather pay for myself."

"You got it."

That taken care of, I ordered my usual, paid up front, and waited until it was ready. Then I carried my food to the booth.

Rin pulled off his headphones. "I guess you have to sing since Leigh isn't serving."

"Ha! Not likely!"

I sipped my strawberry shake, waiting for Rin to get back to drawing, but he just kept watching me. Ugh. I guess we were going to talk about it. Which I had to anyway since I promised Isabella.

"My friend writes articles about music for newspaper club," I started. "That's why we were at the coffeehouse on Friday night." I wanted to make it clear I did not know he'd be there. "You do that a lot?"

"Open mic?" Rin shrugged. "Just twice."

"But you've done that before? Performed in front of a group?"

He shrugged again.

I'd memorized Isabella's short list of questions. I was pretty sure a shrug wouldn't be a satisfying response for her. "Do you write your own music?"

"Yes."

"Really?" I blinked. "You wrote the song you played on Friday?"

He shrugged.

"So, you aren't a fan of secrets and lies," I prompted.

He smiled. "You listened to the lyrics."

"Of course. Who doesn't?" Words were important.

Rin leaned forward. I couldn't see his hands behind the wall of books, but I remembered very clearly what they looked like playing his guitar. "You seem very interested in me all of a sudden."

I refrained from rolling my eyes. "My friend Isabella wants to write an article about you. And about youth open mic." She had an interview with Avi this afternoon.

"Why can't she ask me herself?"

That was a good question. Isabella was a romantic. Did she have ulterior motives, or did she just think Rin and I were friends? "I'm sure she'd be happy to."

"Cool. Do you have her number?" Rin took out his phone. And I gave it to him.

"So, groupies, huh?" I asked.

Rin grinned. "Jealous?"

"Not even!" He could be so arrogant. I was glad he'd

asked for Isabella's number. She could interview him herself.

I got out my homework, and Rin took the hint. He went back to drawing behind his stupid wall. I had more important things to do. I just hoped Olivia would come through for me.

seventeen

Waiting was never easy. Over a week went by with no word from Olivia. I didn't want to be a pest, so I forced myself to keep busy. At least I had a great distraction. It was Tuesday, which meant I was officially a teenager!

"Good morning and happy birthday," Mom said when I walked into the kitchen. "How about dinner at Hirai Ramen tonight?"

My stomach rumbled in approval. "Sounds great!" It wasn't our usual sushi place, but ramen was just as good.

Mom dropped me off at school, and I laughed when I saw my hall locker. It was wrapped in the *New York Times* with a turquoise bow that matched my hair. *Happy birthday, Jenna!* was scrawled in black Sharpie in Keiko's loopy writing across the top.

I opened my locker and then leapt back as a cloud of confetti floated onto the floor.

"Happy birthday!" Keiko appeared next to me, a big smile on her face. She waved a little dustpan and brush.

"You think of everything. Thanks!" I stepped back as Keiko swept up the paper confetti. She went to dump it in the recycling bin, and by the time she'd returned, I had already pulled out a small silver bag from my locker.

"Open it." Keiko was practically jumping up and down.

I pried open the bag and pulled out something small wrapped in blue tissue. Keiko was nearly bursting. I purposely paused, scratched my ear, slooooooowly placed the empty bag back in my locker. Then I straightened the bag, centering it, while still holding the wad of blue tissue.

"Jenna!" Keiko screeched.

I laughed. "Okay, okay!" I peeled back the tissue paper. Nestled inside was a black-and-white beaded bracelet. "Cool," I said. I wasn't much for jewelry, and not to be ungrateful, but I didn't understand why Keiko was so giddy over this.

"It's made from the *New York Times!*" she shouted.

"What?" I took a closer look at the bracelet. From a distance, the beads looked like, well, beads, but when I examined them, I could see that each one was actually rolled newsprint, sprayed with something that made them shiny. I blinked. "This is awesome!"

"Right?"

"Thank you!" I put it on. "I love it!"

Keiko was super pleased with herself. She was good at giving thoughtful gifts. I was glad that things seemed normal between us, despite some of the weirdness and distance over the past couple of weeks. And that I had already figured out what I was getting for her birthday at the end of the month. I was going to do a chocolate-of-the-month club for her, on my own. I'd hand deliver curated chocolate bars every month for a year.

At lunch, the guys sang "Happy Birthday" to me, which was sappy but kind of cool. Keiko presented me with a giant cupcake she baked. This was definitely a better birthday than last year or the year before. I shoved those memories aside. I was having too good a day.

After school, I headed to the diner as usual. When I got there, the booth was empty. Yes! It really was a perfect birthday! I'd finally beaten Rin. Maybe I'd give him a hard time before allowing him to join me.

When I sat down, I noticed a large manila envelope with my name on it staring up at me.

"Happy birthday!" Leigh strode up with a pink milkshake and a plate of cheesy fries.

She sang a line about being wonderful. Leigh's voice was definitely pretty. "This is a special shake I'm calling Glinda and Elphaba's Raspberry Mint shake," Leigh said, placing everything onto the table in front of me. "From *Wicked*? It's raspberry mint ice cream with just a drizzle of chocolate fudge. Get it? Pink and green? On the house!"

"Wow," I said. "Thank you! How did you know it was my birthday?"

"Rin told me."

"He did?" How did *he* know?

The phone by the register rang, and Leigh went to answer it. Where was Rin anyway? He was never late.

I picked up the envelope, wondering what else Leigh got me. She was too generous. Inside was a sheet of paper, and as I pulled it out, I realized that this was not from Leigh. My heart tripped, recognizing Rin's style in the manga drawing.

"Wow." I breathed. He had totally captured my likeness. I was dressed in my regular clothes, jeans and a T-shirt. The shirt had a fierce-looking bear with CUB emblazoned across it. I smirked at the journalism reference. A cape flapped behind me, and I wielded a sword that looked like a giant fountain pen and a shield that looked exactly like my newspaper club notebook. The only color on the drawing was my turquoise hair. Impressive.

I slid the drawing back into the envelope and tucked it into my bag. I didn't want to accidentally spill food on it. Then I took a sip of my birthday shake. It was, of course, delicious. Finally, Rin strolled into the diner from the back hall.

"Hey!" I said when he reached the booth. "Where were you?"

He dumped his backpack onto the bench. "Leigh's husband, Tom, needed a hand carrying some boxes into the kitchen."

Rin sat down and grabbed a handful of fries, popping

them into his mouth. "Happy birthday," he said, his eyes scanning the tabletop.

"Thanks! And thanks for the portrait. It's amazing," I said. "How did you know it was my birthday?"

"I saw your decorated locker."

"You did this drawing today?"

For some reason, his cheeks turned pink. First, he shook his head. Then nodded. And then shook his head again.

"Wait, you did or you didn't?"

And then there it was, the classic Rin shrug. "I've been practicing, you know, drawing female characters. But yeah, I did this one today at lunch."

He'd been practicing drawing female characters? Because of what I'd said?

I liked Super Cub Reporter manga me. "Well, thank you," I said again, running out of words.

Leigh sang the usual *Hamilton* song when she brought Rin his chocolate shake. I really did need to bring Keiko here. Maybe later this week.

And then I made a snap decision. It was my birthday. I was having pretty much the best day in a long time and was feeling lucky. But I was also tired of waiting to hear back from Olivia. I hadn't wanted to bother her—she must be super busy with school and hanging out with Marina. But I needed to know if she'd been able to get me a name. So I'd text her and ask her.

What was the worst that could happen?

eighteen

I tapped out a quick message and was pleased when Olivia texted right back.

> Sorry! I got super busy with school. I got your answer.

I gripped my phone and held my breath, watching the dots, waiting for the rest of her message.

> FYI, my aunt was on the record but doesn't want to be identified as the source.

This was exciting! I felt like a real reporter as I typed back:

> Got it.

> I don't think she'll get in trouble but better to be safe than sorry.

OMG, Olivia. Just spit it out. My leg was jiggling so hard, the whole bench was shaking.

> She won't get fired or anything will she?

> Don't think so. But it would suck if she or the district got sued.

Wow. These rich people obviously had something to hide. They were powerful, entitled, and wealthy. Exactly the kind of people who couldn't be trusted.

> Okay. I promise not to reveal my source. Tell me.

Another long pause while I watched the dots as she typed back.

> Their names are Kenji and Traci Watanabe.

I nearly dropped my phone. Watanabe? I flicked my eyes at Rin, who continued to draw.

I typed Thank you to Olivia and immediately did a web search on my phone, pressing against my legs to try to keep them from bouncing. There! A profile of Kenji Watanabe in USC's alumni magazine. Kenji and Traci Watanabe owned and ran a family business turned international corporation that sold machine parts. I kept skimming until I found what I was looking for. They were the parents to two children, Sarah and Rin.

My legs went still. Rin's family was rich? So rich that they could drop a million dollars just to make a cafeteria pretty? I stared at my phone, the words going blurry.

Rin had pretended not to know about the donation! He'd probably offered to "help me" so he could steer me away from learning about his family. He'd paid for my food to make me feel indebted to him. Mom was right. Dad bought me things so he'd feel less guilty for leaving. And Rin was doing it to make himself feel better about hiding the truth from me. He wrote a song about secrets and lies being bad, but he was the one keeping secrets and telling lies! Anger bubbled inside me until it was a full-on rage boil.

"You!" I pointed at him. "All this time you acted like you wanted to help me. But you just didn't want me to find out!"

Rin looked up from his drawing. "What are you talking about?"

Oh, he was such a great actor. "Your parents are the donors!"

"My what are the what?" His eyebrows were scrunched, making him look confused instead of busted.

"Your parents! Your stupid parents gave a million dollars to the school for the ridiculous cafeteria renovation!"

Rin's face grew stormy. "Did you just call my parents stupid?"

I'd thought his usual scowl was annoying at best, but this look actually scared me a little. I could almost feel his anger coming off in waves. I would not be intimidated! I was onto the story of the century!

"Don't try to deflect! Why did you hide that little piece of information when you knew I needed it for my article?"

"I didn't know!"

"Sure!" I shouted. "Well, I guess if you have the kind of money your family does, a million is nothing! Like pennies!" I lowered my voice. "It's not like the school could've used the money to actually help its students or anything."

Rin's scowl deepened. That fueled me even more. What right did he have to be angry? Because I found him out?

"Why are you here anyway?" I hissed. "I'm sure you can afford to eat at some fancy five-star restaurant!"

Rin grabbed his backpack and jolted out of the booth. He leaned toward me. "You don't know anything about me," he growled, and then stormed out of the diner.

Finally! I had the booth all to myself. I spread my notebook out and started scribbling down the facts. The Watanabes didn't care how they spent their money or think things through enough to really help. They could have gotten the school new computers or funded extra-curricular clubs ... like our newspaper. Why the cafeteria? There had to be a reason, and I was going to dig until I found it. Then I'd write the best investigative piece ever!

I leaned back, feeling satisfied. I was not only going to be the winning entry from PV Middle but in the running to win the scholarship!

"Everything okay?" Leigh asked, concern on her face.

The tips of my ears burned as I realized the entire diner had probably heard me shouting at Rin.

"Um, yeah," I said.

"Happy birthday, Jenna," she said quietly, gathering the empties.

I tried to smile, but it felt forced. "Thank you for the shake and fries."

"Try to have a nice rest of your day." She gave me a sympathetic smile. "I'm sure Rin didn't mean to leave that."

His sketchbook sat abandoned on the table.

"Give it back to him?" she asked.

It was probably better for her to keep it since it wasn't like we were going to hang out again. But my reporter's instinct told me to hold on to it. I tucked it into my messenger bag next to the envelope that held Rin's drawing. Something tugged at me. Why had he given me a gift? Was it to distract me from investigating his family? It didn't make sense. *He* didn't make sense!

I walked home, lost in thought. Why didn't Rin go to a fancy private school? Why was he hanging out at Leigh's diner? He sure wouldn't have to try to win scholarships for college. Not when his family had millions of dollars to spare. Why would he hide that?

One thing was for sure—I was going to get to the heart of this story. Not only for the scholarship, but for me. I deserved to know the truth.

nineteen

I got home earlier than usual. I had over an hour before Mom came home to take me for my birthday dinner. I hurried to my room and opened my laptop. I typed Kenji and Traci Watanabe into my search engine. This time I slowed down, carefully reading everything I found and taking lots of notes.

AkiWata Corporation made and sold parts for machinery. The founder was Akira Watanabe, Rin's grandfather. He had invented a special heat-resistant spring originally used in cameras, but the company expanded to manufacture other parts. I jotted down a note to myself to see if these parts were used in school cafeterias. Maybe they funded the renovation to encourage other schools to buy their products. Could it all be just a promotion for AkiWata? I kept reading. The company, now run by Rin's father, Kenji, was privately owned and hugely successful, meaning the Watanabes were richer than rich.

I clicked to another article that was more recent. Rin's sister, Sarah, had graduated with honors from a private high school and was now a freshman majoring in business at Harvard. I knew I'd never be able to go to a college like Harvard. Mom couldn't afford that for sure.

I typed Rin's name into my search engine, but nothing came up other than the articles I'd already found.

"Oh, birthday girl!" Mom called. "You ready to go?"

I hadn't even heard her come home. With a sigh, I closed my laptop. Once again, I had more questions than answers.

~

When my alarm went off the next morning, I hit snooze four times.

"Jenna?" Mom said, opening my door. "You're still asleep? I have to leave in ten minutes."

That got me out of bed. I got dressed, grabbing my Asian American Girl Club T-shirt. After I brushed my teeth and ran a brush through my hair, I barely had time to grab a Pop-Tart before hopping in the Honda. Mom had already backed it out of the garage.

"You okay?" Mom asked.

"I stayed up late doing an assignment," I mumbled, trying to force myself awake.

"On your birthday? Wow. I'm proud of you, Jenna." Mom beamed at me. I hadn't told her about the Orange County Junior Journalism Scholarship because I didn't want to get her hopes up.

I felt good about the draft I'd written so far. I was missing the key element, though. I had to have proof that the Watanabes had an agenda. I mean, it was bad enough that they'd wasted money on something so frivolous, but that wouldn't win me the scholarship. I needed time to do more research. I was sure I'd discover something important.

Once I had that, maybe, just maybe, I'd share my article with Ms. Fontes. She'd offered to help newspaper club members with their contest entries. I was feeling pretty confident that I wouldn't need help, but it wouldn't hurt to have Ms. Fontes know how awesome my entry was. I was feeling so confident that I'd written and saved a draft of the email I'd send to her when my article was ready.

I couldn't remember what time I'd gone to bed, but I'd been researching and writing until at least three a.m. Good thing I didn't have any tests today. I would not be at my best.

By the time lunch came around, I felt a little more like myself.

While the guys got into a heated debate over a video game, Keiko and I caught up.

"How's your article coming?" Keiko asked me.

"Pretty good! I think I have most of the information I need."

"That's great, Jenna," Keiko said. "I've missed you."

"Yeah, sorry that I haven't been around."

"It's okay. I know this scholarship is important."

"Once I'm done with it, we can hang out on Tuesdays and Thursdays again." At least, I hoped she'd still want to.

"Can't wait!" Keiko smiled. "And Mom still can't find our Scrabble set, so we can play something else again on Saturday."

That got the guys' attention. They whooped and cheered like they'd won a trophy. Keiko and I laughed. It felt good to laugh with her again.

"Hey, isn't that your friend from newspaper club?" Keiko asked.

Isabella stood at the bottom of the bleachers, waving to me. I marched down to meet her.

"Hey, what's up?" I asked.

Isabella grinned. "I had to tell you as soon as I found out."

"What?"

"Ms. Fontes got approval for us to do a digital newspaper next year!"

My grin matched Isabella's. "Really? That's incredible!"

"We're going to try to raise funds this semester to cover some costs. Plus, if we raise enough money, there's a cool journalism conference we all might be able to attend next year!"

"That would be awesome!"

"We're voting today on what fundraisers we'll run. Come back, Jenna. It's not the same without you. And you know you want to be part of creating our school's first paper!"

Isabella was 100 percent right. There was no way I was going to miss it. But I didn't know how Ms. Fontes would react if I just showed up again like nothing had happened.

"She's been asking about you," Isabella said, studying my face. I would be a lousy poker player. "Just come back. It's a club. Everyone and anyone is allowed to join. She can't stop you from being in it."

Couldn't she, though?

After school, I paced up and down the hallway that led to her classroom. I was going to go in. I really was.

But I ducked back behind the corner when I saw Elliot. He was first as always. I counted to ten and peeked. Carlos and Thea followed and then Isabella and Caitlin. It looked like they were getting tight. I wondered if they were sharing a table now. Everyone was gelling as a team. Without me.

I mentally kicked myself. I had no right to feel jealous. I was the one who'd left.

Finally, Ms. Fontes came down the hall with her usual travel mug of iced coffee. I rushed to cut her off while she was still far enough away that no one could overhear our conversation.

"Jenna!" Ms. Fontes seriously looked happy to see me. Relief and hope flooded me. "I've been wondering what happened to you. Is everything okay?"

"Yeah, um, I had some, um, things come up." Ugh. I was

not good at concealing the truth. "Actually, I was stuck on that personal essay. I wanted to work on something else."

Ms. Fontes looked solemn. "I suspected something like that. Look, Jenna, I'm not going to force you to write that essay. This is a club, and I want it to be useful but also fun. You're very talented, as evidenced by your article. Is that what you're submitting with the scholarship application?"

"What?"

"The story on the cafeteria donation. It's interesting."

My ears flamed, and I gripped my messenger bag. "What are you talking about?"

Ms. Fontes cocked her head at me. "Did you not intend to send me your article this morning?"

I closed my eyes and took a deep breath. "Oh, no. I mean, yes, eventually I wanted to share it with you, but that was just a working draft. I must have hit send instead of saving it." I was mortified. While I was proud of what I had so far, it was nowhere near ready to share.

Ms. Fontes nodded. "Well, it's a good start. It did seem to be lacking some focus. I'd be happy to discuss it with you. That is, if you'd like some feedback."

I didn't want her to think I wasn't able to take criticism. "I'd love that."

"And in case you haven't heard," she said. "We have been approved to put out a digital paper next year."

I wished I were able to twist the truth. I didn't want her to know that this was the reason I was returning. "Um, yeah. Isabella mentioned it."

"Good." Ms. Fontes waved her mug toward the room. "Shall we?"

When we walked into the room, all activity stopped.

"Jenna! You're back!" Isabella stood and waved to me from our table. Caitlin and Laurel were sitting there, too. I joined them. Ben and Brody called out to me. The sight of the messy bulletin board, the mock layout on Ms. Fontes's desk, and the ancient computers filled me with warmth. It felt like coming home.

"Good afternoon, reporters," Ms. Fontes said. She smiled my way, and I was grateful she didn't make a big deal about me returning.

"As you know, by the end of this semester, I will be assigning roles for next year's paper. You will have to be flexible, however, and pitch in where needed since we won't have a full staff. This means that even if you are assigned to be news editor, you may be asked to step in to write a movie review. There is also a good chance we'll have more members next year."

There was an uproar of protests.

"That's not fair," Thea said. "We've been working hard all year, and a new person will get to just come along and get choice assignments?"

Ms. Fontes looked stern. "This is a club. That means learning, teamwork, and inclusivity."

We all got quiet.

"Will there be an editor in chief?" Elliot asked the question that was top in my mind.

"We'll see," she said. "Let's focus on doing the best we can to prepare for this exciting endeavor."

Ms. Fontes had taken suggestions for fundraisers during the last meeting and written them on the board for us to vote on. Fortunately, the walkathon was voted down quickly. That did not sound fun. And as much as a school carnival appealed to all of us, we didn't have the time or people to pull that off. The idea that won would provide the quickest results without a ton of work.

"Weekly bake sale it is," Ms. Fontes said. "Is there a day that would work best for everyone?"

"How about Mondays?" Isabella suggested. "That way we can bake on a Sunday. I'll bet students would be happy to buy a treat to start off the week. And bonus! Monday is Valentine's Day! A perfect time to sell sweets."

I used every bit of willpower not to look at Elliot. We had once had a great discussion on the ridiculousness of Valentine's Day and had promised each other we wouldn't acknowledge it. That was one promise neither of us would have trouble keeping.

As everyone got busy making a schedule, Ms. Fontes came over to me. "Jenna, while you don't have to write the personal essay, should you ever feel inspired, I would be more than happy to read it."

I nodded. There was no way I'd ever write the thing, and I was glad to be off the hook.

"Shall we discuss your scholarship entry?"

"Great!"

I pulled up a chair to Ms. Fontes's desk. I noticed Elliot watching, and that made me feel smug. He probably thought I was already angling to be editor in chief. Well, let him.

For once, all the pieces were clicking into place. Everything was finally going right!

twenty

For the rest of the week, I threw myself into research mode. I went straight home after school or club so I could use my own laptop and our fast Wi-Fi. Working on this article was more important than my feelings of being alone in the house. I was so focused that I barely missed going to the diner, and I definitely didn't miss Rin. I didn't miss the way his pen moved across the paper, or the way he pushed his glasses up with his finger, or the way his hair sometimes fell across his eyes. I didn't think about him at all.

I found tons of articles on Rin's dad, Kenji, and the conferences he was speaking at, and a mention in *Forbes*.

Both of Rin's parents made frequent appearances at Los Angeles openings of museums and restaurants, and just last week Rin's mom had been photographed with a chef at a fancy restaurant opening.

Elliot kept trying to figure out what I was working on. Sometimes he reminded me of my dad but not in a good way. Dad had abandoned me. Elliot had, too. And both of them thought it was okay to come in and out of my life whenever it suited them. Luckily, Elliot was easy to ignore.

"Do you want to come over for the movie tonight?" Doug asked me at lunch on Friday.

Keiko looked up from her sandwich. We had hardly spent any time together outside of game night. I missed her, but I had more important things to do.

"I can't."

Keiko's shoulders drooped, but she didn't try to convince me to join them.

It was just as well. I had a month to get this article in perfect shape, and I couldn't do that if I didn't have the information I needed. There was only one way I could find out why Rin's parents had donated the money, and this time I wasn't going to be discouraged.

"Jenna Sakai, nice to see you again." Mr. Kim looked up from his screen as I poked my head into his office after the last bell rang.

"Hi, Mr. Kim." I plopped into the chair across from him and made a big show of taking out my notebook and pen. I wasn't going anywhere. "I have a few more questions for you about the article I'm writing."

His smile faltered. Good. If I was making him uncomfortable, then I was onto something.

"I know that Kenji and Traci Watanabe paid for the cafeteria renovation," I said.

"I'm impressed."

Just wait and see how much more impressed you are going to be, I thought. "Thanks, Mr. Kim. Now that you don't have to worry about revealing their identities, I was hoping you could tell me the truth about a few other things."

Mr. Kim's smile disappeared completely. "Jenna, I don't think you understand what this donation was really all about."

"True," I said. "That's why I'm coming to you."

He paused. "Since this is for your scholarship application, I think it's best that you find the information without my input. I'm a judge, and it might be seen as an unfair advantage."

Right. He was trying to get rid of me again. But I wouldn't be easily pushed off. "I can see that, but—"

"I'll give you a little hint, though," Mr. Kim interrupted. "Look more closely at Traci Watanabe. I mean very closely."

Interesting! I scribbled her name in my notebook and circled it three times. That was a good lead. I didn't expect him to tell me much more. "Thank you, Mr. Kim."

When I got home, I was surprised to see Keiko waiting for me. I checked my phone and sure enough she'd texted that she was coming.

"Hey," I said, taking out my key to open the door. "Sorry! I didn't check my phone till just now."

"Oh." Keiko looked relieved. "I thought maybe you were ignoring me."

"What? No!"

"Okay." Keiko followed me into the house. After we both took off our shoes, we headed to my room and sat on my bed, backs against the wall. "What's going on? I feel like we haven't talked in forever."

I started to shrug but then caught myself. The gesture belonged to Rin, and I did not want to think of him. I was so annoyed and frustrated by the way he'd tricked me that suddenly I couldn't stop the words from pouring out of me.

I spilled everything to Keiko—what I learned from Olivia and Mr. Kim for my article, how we were going to get a digital paper next year and I was determined to beat Elliot out for editor, and how Rin had lied to me.

"What a jerk," Keiko said, her hands turning into fists. "Did he admit it?"

"No," I said. "But how could he not know his parents had donated that much money?"

Keiko cocked her head at me.

"What?"

"Did you give him a chance to explain? Or defend himself?"

Whose side was she on? "He stormed off! That's guilty behavior!"

Keiko nodded. One of the qualities I appreciated about her was that she didn't like conflict. She stood and stretched, changing the subject. "What's that?"

Keiko pointed at the manga portrait of me. I had it propped up on my desk.

"Oh. Rin drew it."

Keiko sat at my desk and gingerly picked it up. "It's you! And it's amazing! You didn't tell me he was an artist."

I hadn't told her much about him at all. "It was a birthday gift," I mumbled.

"What?" Keiko squealed. "He drew you a birthday present? Jenna! This is huge!"

"No, it isn't." I got up and took the drawing from Keiko and shoved it in a drawer. "He was trying to distract me from finding out the truth about his parents."

"That doesn't make sense. Besides, if he's as rich as you say he is, why not buy you something flashy and expensive? This seems so much more personal."

Exactly. He thought one sweet gesture would have me falling at his feet like all those giggling girls at the coffeehouse and forgetting I was digging up dirt on his family. Which was why he wasn't to be trusted.

But I knew that look on Keiko's face. She was no longer angry on my behalf. She was looking for the good, for the silver lining in all this. "You don't think he was just... being nice?"

"Rin and I are not friends, Keiko," I said. "Mr. Kim gave me a lead, and I'm going to follow it. Whatever it is, I'm using it. If Rin's family is hiding something, it's my responsibility to report it."

"Fine."

"Keiko, don't be upset with me."

She sighed. "I'm not. I just want you to be objective about this."

"I *am* being objective! Otherwise wouldn't I kill the story to protect Rin?"

"I thought you said you weren't friends."

"We aren't! This whole conversation is stupid."

Keiko went silent. But I didn't need her approval. She didn't understand how important this was to me. Why reporting the truth mattered so much. She never had to deal with parents who kept things from her. Her parents had never let their version of events drive a wedge between them. Perceptions could be twisted, but facts were concrete. So telling the truth was important. It was times like this that I missed Elliot the most.

Keiko looked at her phone. "I have to get going to

Doug's. Are you sure you don't want to come? His mom makes amazing meals."

I shook my head. "I have work to do."

"Okay. But just remember..." Keiko paused. "Sometimes the truth isn't only one thing."

She left and an uneasy feeling weighed on me, but I shook it off. When it came to Rin Watanabe, I had to be objective, focused, and heartless.

twenty-one

I spent the entire weekend researching with the exception of a couple of hours on Sunday afternoon. I'd asked Keiko to help me bake for the newspaper club fundraiser. I was relieved she'd agreed, and even though our conversation had been slightly stilted, at least she came over.

On Sunday night, I ate a PB&J sandwich for dinner in my room so I could keep researching.

"Are you sure you don't want to watch a movie with me?" Mom asked when she came to get my empty plate.

"I'm sure," I said, jotting down more notes.

"Can't that wait?" Mom asked.

I spun to face her. "Excuse me? Aren't you the one who is always on me to study and get great grades?"

Mom smiled. "Yes, but you can take a break once in a while. Come spend some time with your mom. I have a little free time right now."

I scowled. "I never guilt-trip you when you have to work. What I'm doing is important."

Mom sighed but left me to it. I closed the door so she wouldn't bother me again.

I'd spent the first part of the weekend reading about what Traci Watanabe wore to events and where she got her diamonds, but eventually I found something interesting. Traci Watanabe held no official title or role at the AkiWata Corporation, but she was the founder and sole chairperson of the Feed Schools Foundation. And she worked hard to keep it completely separate from the corporation and her family. Rin's dad wasn't mentioned anywhere on the foundation's website. But lots of other stuff was.

The charity provided funding to supplement the free lunch program in California. It also helped schools hire trained cooks for their kitchen staff.

My mind was spinning. Rin's mom ran a foundation

to help feed hungry kids? That was pretty great. But it didn't mean that everything the Watanabes did was great. I dug around the website trying to find out about our cafeteria renovation, but there was no mention of the donation. That was suspicious for sure. They were trying to keep it quiet as I suspected, but why?

PV Middle could definitely use the money, but we weren't in real need the way the Title I schools the foundation usually helped were. Was the donation some kind of tax write-off? Or a way to hide the money they made so they wouldn't have to pay taxes on it? I kept reading, but all the articles I found about the foundation were full of praise. Gah!

I rubbed my eyes and glanced at my clock. It was two a.m. I had to get some sleep, but I felt like I was so close to finding out vital information. It felt just out of reach.

I blinked wearily, leaning back in my desk chair. My eyes caught on the manga drawing Rin had done of me. I'd taken it back out of the drawer the minute Keiko had left my room, and set it back up on my desk. It wasn't that I was attached to it because Rin had drawn it. I loved it because it showed me as Super Cub Reporter. It was inspirational.

So inspirational, I realized I'd overlooked the best source I'd ever find.

"That's it, Jenna," I said out loud with disgust. "If only you had access to a Watanabe family member who could give you the scoop!" I should never have yelled at Rin. I'd let my anger get the better of me. A good reporter would have taken that unexpected information and turned it to her advantage. Instead of accusing Rin, I could have asked him for information.

Maybe it wasn't too late. If I apologized for snapping at him, he might be willing to tell me about his parents. And I had to admit, it *was* possible Rin hadn't known about the donation. My parents never discussed finances with me. The only reason I knew anything about them at all was because of the shouting matches they had had before the divorce.

I hadn't been to the diner in days. But I didn't want to wait till after school to talk to Rin. And then it hit me.

His sketchbook! It was still in my bag. I'd been so focused on research that I'd almost forgotten about it. Now it would come in handy!

I had no idea what Rin's personal email address was, but I did know his school account.

From: **Jenna Sakai** <jreports@memail.com>

To: **Rin Watanabe** <rin.watanabe@pvms.org>

Subject: **Your sketchbook**

Hi! I have your sketchbook. I haven't looked at it in case you're worried about that. Let's meet up by the front steps before school tomorrow so I can return it to you.

—Jenna

I hit send. All I had to do now was wait.

twenty-two

The next morning, I woke up with purpose. Rin had to know—or at least be able to find out—something that would give my article the heat it needed to be a really great story. And I was going to do whatever I needed to find out.

I waited in front of the school until ten minutes before the bell rang. He never showed up. I didn't want to get marked tardy, so I went to social studies feeling frustrated. I wanted to swing by the music room during lunch, but I'd signed up for the bake sale, so talking to Rin would have to wait.

I headed to the cafeteria carrying the chocolate fudge brownies Keiko and I had baked. I'd insisted on non-heart-themed brownies for the Valentine's Day bake sale but had helped her top the strawberry-frosted cupcakes she made for Conner with a candy heart and a chocolate kiss. They were works of art.

When I got to the cafeteria, I nearly dropped the brownies. Elliot was sitting behind the bake sale table. The chair next to him was empty. I was sure I'd signed up for a time slot with Isabella to prevent this awkward situation from happening.

I plopped the plate onto the tabletop amid pink-frosted cupcakes and heart-shaped cookies.

"What are you doing here?" I asked. "And where's Isabella?"

"She traded with me," Elliot said.

"Why?"

"Because I asked."

I frowned. "Why?"

"Sit down, Jenna. You're blocking the table."

I complied but scooted my chair away from Elliot.

Lucky for me we got busy almost instantly. We had a line of people waiting to buy Valentine's Day treats. By an unspoken agreement, Elliot pitched and sold, and I handled the cash.

A slim hand with a perfect manicure and pale-pink-painted nails handed me a five-dollar bill. I looked up, and there was Audrey surrounded by her two new besties and three guys who hung back behind them. The girls wore matching pink sweaters.

"Jenna! How cute that you're selling cookies," Audrey said in what I knew was her fake-friendly voice. "Hi, Elliot!"

Elliot blinked at Audrey and her friends, and his cheeks flushed to match Audrey's sweater. I snatched the money out of Audrey's hand and shoved three dollars back at her.

"Too bad you're single on Valentine's Day," Audrey said, flashing her eyes at Elliot meaningfully. I guess gossip traveled even from the outer rims of popularity to the inner circles. But I wanted to report the news; I didn't want to *be* the news! And besides, I'd never cared about having a boyfriend the way Audrey did.

"It's fine," I muttered, my jaw clenched tight.

Audrey laughed. "Sure," she said. Then she and her minions strutted away.

Fifteen minutes before the bell rang, we ran out of baked goods.

"If we can keep up sales like that, we'll have enough to fund the paper easily," Elliot said.

I gathered the leftover napkins.

"We make a good team, you and me," Elliot said.

I straightened the cash and closed the box.

"I miss working with you." Elliot moved his chair closer. "How is your scholarship article going? What were you working on again?"

"I didn't say. What are *you* working on?"

Elliot smiled. "I have a lead on an interesting situation at school, but I'm still looking into it."

I wasn't surprised he was being vague. I wasn't revealing anything to him, either.

"You're going to do a great job, I'll bet," he said. "I can't wait to see your story."

I narrowed my eyes at him, suspicion overtaking me. "I'm not showing it to you."

"Why not? We always share our writing with each other."

"We're not together anymore!"

"That doesn't mean we can't *work* together. You're the only one in the club who's even close to being as good a writer as I am. There's no reason we can't help make each other's stories better. Because one of us will win the PV Middle cash award for sure. Though, let's face it, it will probably be me."

Gah! Condescending. Why had I thought his confidence was an endearing trait?

"Aw, come on, Jenna, don't be all angry." Elliot reached into his jacket pocket and handed me a pink heart-shaped cookie. "Truce? Happy Valentine's Day."

What was he doing? We'd made fun of Valentine's Day! Why give me a cookie? Why give me anything?

I bolted up and shoved the cashbox into Elliot's arms, squishing the cookie against him. "Take this to Ms. Fontes."

Then I spun on my heels and got out of there as fast as I could. I did not want to talk with Elliot. I did not want him to shower me with false praise. I did not want to hear his lies.

"Jenna! Wait!"

I shut out his voice as I sped up. I might have left him behind, but the anger followed me the rest of the day.

After school, Rin's sketchbook tucked safely in my bag, I was determined to find him. I could go to the diner, but I'd been waiting all day. I wanted answers now! I headed to the front of the main building where pickup and drop-off was. I'd asked around and learned that he got a ride to and from school. That's how he always beat me to the diner, the cheat!

Throngs of students milled around on the front lawn. I stood at the top of the steps, searching, thinking it would be impossible to find Rin in the crowd. But then I saw him—that black backpack, that confident saunter, those headphones. Rin.

I ignored the pounding of my heart and the fact that my face grew warm. I took off down the steps and speed-walked over to him, cutting him off as he approached a silver Lexus.

I stopped in front of him. He started to sidestep around me without even looking up.

"Rin," I said loudly, just in case he was actually listening to music on his headphones.

That stopped him in his tracks. His eyes met mine, and my breath hitched.

"Did you get my email?"

"I got it," he said in that low, arrogant voice.

"You didn't answer." I reached into my messenger bag and pulled out his sketchbook. "This is yours." As Rin held out his hand, I continued. "But will you answer a few questions first?"

Rin shook his head. "You know what? I don't want it." He pushed past me and got into the car.

I stood there, watching the Lexus pull away, Rin's sketchbook still in my hand.

twenty-three

When I got home, I went straight to my room. I pulled out Rin's sketchbook and placed it on my desk.

If a real reporter got ahold of something that might help with an investigation, they wouldn't hesitate. This sketchbook could reveal important information for my article. I ran my hand over the smooth black cover. I wasn't breaking the law. Rin knew I had it. I'd told him I hadn't looked at it, but that was then. Whatever I did with it now was fair game.

Still, my stomach did a weird dipping thing, like I was on a roller coaster. I took a deep breath and opened the book.

The first page was blank except for a date, December 17, which weirdly enough was the day Elliot and I broke up. I traced the date with my finger, recalling the anger that coursed through me as I walked home from school. But something had happened on the walk. For the first half, I was on the verge of either crying or screaming. But with every step that followed, I erased every feeling I ever had about Elliot. And by the time I got home, I felt hollowed—he was just ... gone.

On the next page I saw a manga-style drawing of a guy and some sort of cute alien creature. It had pointy ears and antennae and floated on a disc. In fact, there were lots of superheroes and warriors, some with alien companions. They were pretty cool but all male. Every page was dated. Rin drew almost every day.

The page marked December 30 was a completely different style. Instead of a cartoon, it was realistic, and instead of black ink, it was drawn in pencil. A dinner scene. As I peered closer, I realized it was Rin's family. I recognized his parents and sister from my online research. The whole drawing looked soft and warm. His parents were smiling as they looked at Rin's sister, who seemed to be telling a story. One of her hands was waving. There was food on the table. I recognized a plate of tamago, my favorite Japanese-style omelet. But the dishes were fancy with intricate flower patterns and the glassware looked like crystal. Maybe it was Christmas dinner. Or maybe that's how they ate all the time. I felt like I was peering into the window of Rin's house. It made my heart ache—I never got to have family meals like that anymore. I stared at that page for a long time.

Then it was back to more of Rin's manga drawings. A few pages later, I recognized the sketches he'd shown me at the diner. But then I saw something entirely different. Rin's drawings were usually original. But this character I recognized immediately. It was Kagome, the female hero of the manga I had told Rin I'd read. The next five pages were filled with drawings of all the different girl characters from the series. Rin had started drawing them after I'd pointed out he only drew boys. It amazed me that he'd listened. And it made me feel weirdly happy.

The next page was Rin's attempt to draw a female manga character of his own creation. It was a rough pencil sketch and looked a little like one of Rumiko Takahashi's characters in modern clothing. Jeans, T-shirt, and sneakers. As I turned the pages, the sketches grew more detailed and Rin stopped using pencil and switched to ink. It was kind of cool to see his process of creating a character.

When I turned to the next page, I froze.

I stared at an image of me. Not manga me but like that scene Rin had drawn of his family at the dinner table, a realistic drawing in pencil. I was sitting in the diner booth, staring down at my newspaper club notebook, my pen in motion, spinning in my hand. I stared at the page for so long that the drawing was going to be forever seared in my brain.

I lifted the next page, not sure what to expect. In this one, I was staring toward the door of the diner, my face in a scowl. Then came a drawing of me sipping my milkshake followed by one of me actually smiling, although it was more of a smirk. These drawings were sparse with little to no background, like he'd done a quick sketch and then worked on them later.

After that, the rest of the pages were of manga me. Finally, I got about halfway through the sketchbook, where tiny pieces of paper were caught in the spiral binding. This was the page he had ripped out and given to me for my birthday.

I felt the surprising joy of getting that gift from him all over again. And I started to realize that maybe he wasn't the arrogant jerk I'd thought he was. He'd listened. He'd taken time and effort to draw female characters. And the tips of my ears got warm as I thought of all those sketches of me.

I was slightly offended at this invasion of privacy. How dare he draw me without permission. But I had to admit I was mostly flattered. Rin saw me. And he wasn't asking anything of me other than to just be me.

Hmmm. For all the time we had spent together in the diner, I didn't know much about him. Sure, he didn't really know anything about me, either, but that was okay. He didn't need to know anything about me. I, on the other hand, prided myself on being a great reporter. And reporters ask questions. I should have done a better job of getting to know Rin. If I had, I'd have known about his parents and the foundation already. And maybe more.

A wave of something dark roiled through me.

I'm not using him, I told myself. *That's not the kind of reporter I want to be.*

But I should have been more curious and asked

more questions. It's how you treated friends. And even not-quite-friends like Rin.

I closed the book. I hated to be wrong, but I also respected the truth when I saw it. I had no right to hold Rin's personal property hostage for my own gain. I shouldn't have gone through his sketchbook. My newspaper club notebook wasn't a diary, but I still wouldn't want to share the contents with anyone. The thought of prying eyes made me angry. As much as I wanted information, I couldn't force it.

And the truth—the real truth—was that I had to genuinely apologize to Rin, with no strings attached.

twenty-four

Mr. Kim didn't seem happy to see me. No smile, just a weary wave of his hand to allow me into his office the next day.

"Thank you, Mr. Kim, for the lead," I began with a big smile. "I found the Feed Schools Foundation."

He leaned back in his chair. "I'm glad. Now do you have what you need for your article?"

"Just one more thing," I said, not missing how Mr. Kim pressed his lips together like he was holding in a sigh. "I couldn't find any mention of the PV Middle donation on the site."

"That's because the donation didn't quite come

through the foundation." Mr. Kim sounded resigned, like I'd beaten him down. That made me feel triumphant. I had what it took to be a great investigative journalist!

I opened my notebook. My pen poised and ready, I nodded to Mr. Kim.

This time he did sigh out loud. I could almost read the thought bubble over his head—*I give up*. "It was a pet project. As you know by now, renovating cafeterias is not something the foundation does. Traci Watanabe is on the school board, so she knew we were trying to raise funds to replace our old kitchen equipment. She offered to cover the renovation personally. The foundation only paid for the expanded lunch program and additional kitchen staff."

My pen flew across the page. This wasn't at all what I was expecting. "What do you mean 'expanded lunch program'? I thought the foundation only did that for Title I schools."

Mr. Kim gave me an appraising look. "You are good at research, Jenna, I have to give you that much. It's true that we aren't a Title I school, but that doesn't mean we don't have students who are part of the free meal program. If not for the donation, we might have had to close our cafeteria down until we could afford to replace the kitchen equipment. Students who rely on the program would have had to go without."

I scribbled everything he said into my notebook, my mind spinning. "If Traci Watanabe was doing something generous, why did she make the donation anonymous?" I asked.

"Because she didn't want anyone to misunderstand the foundation's purpose. They're focused strictly on access to nutrition, not construction. But this is the middle school both the Watanabes and their kids attended, so they wanted to help."

It was my turn to sigh. I twirled my pen.

"Jenna, I appreciate your hard work here," Mr. Kim said. "What Traci and her foundation did was admirable. Her donation helped not only the school but students, particularly those on the lunch program."

He stood. "The bell is about to ring. I wish you luck with your entry."

This information changed everything. If what Mr. Kim said was true, the Watanabes hadn't done anything wrong and my story was sunk. It would be hard to write about the donation without talking about how it had helped students in need, and feel-good stories didn't usually win awards. But a reporter couldn't just pick and choose facts to spin an article.

Still, I had to chase down every lead. Which meant I had to talk to one more person.

~

After school, I waited at the curb for Rin, shielded by a big magnolia tree. I was going to apologize and return his sketchbook. I'd gotten too competitive, and it had blinded me to the truth.

But at least I knew how to apologize! Unlike Elliot, who never thought he was wrong. I still couldn't believe he'd wanted to spend time with me at the bake sale, as if everything would be forgiven and forgotten. He'd never apologized for being pushy and condescending. Or for taking credit for work that wasn't his. Or for abandoning me.

I waited and waited, but the Lexus never showed up. Of course, it didn't. This day was the worst. I texted Keiko to let her know I wouldn't be making it to the park to watch the boys' basketball game. I'd been canceling on her a lot lately. But I'd make it up to her once I was done writing this article. If I ever wrote this article. It wasn't looking good for me right now.

I went to the diner. My booth was empty. Disappointment filled me.

"Jenna!" Leigh hurried over, a smile on her face. "It's good to see you. I was starting to worry about you two."

"Worry?" I stood in the middle of the diner. "Where's Rin?"

"He hasn't been in since you two had your spat," Leigh said, wringing her hands. "I hope he's okay. Do you want your usual shake?"

"Sure, thanks. And some cheesy Fetch Fries, too?" I would wait. Maybe Rin would still show up. In the meantime, I'd write up some questions to ask him now that I had new information.

But it was hard to focus. I kept glancing over to where Rin usually sat and then remembering that I was alone.

I sipped my shake and nibbled on the cheesy fries. While they still tasted good, it wasn't the same, eating by myself. Could it be that I missed Rin? I didn't even know him. How could I miss someone I wasn't friends with?

Caring about people only led to getting hurt. My

parents showed me that big-time. And Elliot had rein-forced it. Why did I keep thinking about him? Gah! I blamed it on the bake-sale fiasco.

I finished all my homework and even read ahead in my social studies textbook. When I was done, I left cash on the table and packed up.

"You'll be back, right?" Leigh asked.

"Of course." It felt hypocritical to stop coming just because Rin wasn't here. I'd wanted the booth to myself, and now I had it. Be careful what you wish for.

I was struck by a wave of loneliness. Being alone was good, but only when it was by choice. Could it be I was making bad choices? I was so confused.

On my walk home, I texted Keiko.

> Hey. Are we okay?

Keiko responded immediately.

> Sorry for bailing on you so much.

> I get it. You're working on that scholarship.

> But?

No buts.

> You think I'm being too reporter-y.

I'm on your side. Always. Did you talk to Rin?

> No. But I will.

Keiko didn't ask if I was going to apologize and make up. She didn't give me grief for wanting to interrogate him for my article. If I told her what Mr. Kim had revealed, she'd never say "I told you so." She was always there for me. And even though I pushed her away, I didn't want her going anywhere. She was pretty much the only person I could count on.

> Keiko . . .

Yeah?

> Thanks for being a good friend.

Keiko sent a thumbs-up and a heart emoji.

I got home and pulled out my key, but when I went to insert it into the lock, I heard something I hadn't heard in a long time. I pressed my ear to the door. Yep. It was Mom. Shouting. Angrily.

I turned the key and opened the door a crack. Her voice blasted from the kitchen.

"It's a school night! Do you hear me? This is rude and selfish! Why are you springing it on me now?"

Um. Okay. She used that voice with only one person. I thought I'd never have to hear her yell like that again after Dad moved out. I sighed. I might as well go inside. It wasn't like she was going to get off the phone anytime soon.

Just as I nudged the door open a crack, I heard Dad's voice.

"Beth, just calm down."

I flung open the door and slammed it behind me as I kicked off my shoes. My left shoe flew off and banged into the wall. I ran into the kitchen.

There was Mom, standing at the stove, her arms crossed and her face in an angry scowl. And there was my dad. Not on speakerphone. In person.

twenty-five

"Jenna!"

Dad's smile was like a million hugs, if we were a hugging kind of family.

"What are you doing here?" I asked, trying to keep my voice neutral.

"That's what I was asking." Mom's voice, on the other hand, was sharp.

I wanted to stop her from saying more, but I had learned that nothing could keep my parents from fighting. Then Mom saw my face, and I was surprised when she dropped her arms and her angry scowl.

"I'm here on business," Dad said, giving Mom a

pointed look. "It was last minute, so I didn't get a chance to let you know earlier. And I'm heading back first thing tomorrow morning, so I wanted to see if you were free for dinner right now."

"Like I said, it's a school night." Mom's voice had lost its sharp edge.

"I've already done all my homework." I said a silent thanks to Rin for not showing up at the diner after all.

I watched Mom's face play out her internal struggle. She had no good reason to keep me home other than to annoy Dad. I geared myself up to argue but didn't need to.

"I want her home by eight," Mom said. She picked up her coffee mug and left the kitchen without another word. I knew she wasn't mad at me, but I couldn't help the guilt that bubbled up inside me. Like I'd chosen sides.

"Where to?" Dad asked, following me to the front door.

I retrieved my shoe from across the room. "Our usual?"

"Las Barcas it is!"

The Mexican restaurant was over in Huntington

Beach, but it was our go-to place back when Dad still lived here.

"How was your birthday?" Dad asked.

"Good." It had been one of my better birthdays, until the fallout with Rin. "Thanks for the birthday check," I said as Dad maneuvered his rental car onto the 405. Of course, we hit traffic right away.

"I hope you bought yourself something nice." Dad's car inched forward.

I shook my head. That two hundred dollars went right into the bank.

Dad glanced at me and wrinkled his forehead. "No? Jenna, it's a gift. Spend it."

A gift with strings. Mom had huffed with annoyance when she'd seen the check. "He's trying to buy your love," she'd said. I hadn't understood. I mean, I already loved him—why would he need to buy it? But yeah, now I got it. He hoped I'd choose sides. He hoped I'd choose him. Why would I when he so obviously didn't choose me?

"I put it in my savings account," I said.

Dad honked his horn as someone tried to pull into our lane. They swerved back, barely missing us. "Are you saving for something big? A car? We can talk about getting you one when you turn sixteen."

"A car?" I almost scoffed. "Um, no. I'm saving for college!"

Dad changed lanes. "Why? Didn't your mom tell you I'm paying for it?"

"Wait. What?"

We took the exit and pulled out of traffic.

"Hang on, kiddo. Let's finish this conversation at dinner."

I jiggled my leg nervously as Dad pulled into the crowded Las Barcas parking lot and found a spot right by the entrance. We hopped out of the car, walked into the small restaurant, and got in line. I glanced at the menu board even though I always got the fish tacos.

After Dad put in our orders, I grabbed the paper tray of tortilla chips and went to get a table while he scooped our favorite green salsa into little plastic cups. When he sat down, I jumped back into the conversation where we'd left off.

"Dad? College?"

He scooped salsa with a chip and crunched. "Mmm. I

have missed this place." He gave me a teasing grin. "And you. I've missed you, kid."

"I miss you, too, Dad. Now stop deflecting."

"Always the hard-hitting reporter, never discouraged." He sighed. "I don't want to get in the middle of whatever you think you know."

"Dad!" I was exasperated. Parents were exhausting!

"I already told your mom I'd pay for college."

"But Mom was complaining about how she couldn't afford it. She told me I needed to get scholarships and financial aid. She said you weren't paying for any of it and that it wasn't part of the divorce agreement."

Dad narrowed his eyes, looking as angry as I'd ever seen him. "Your mom told you that? Why is she discussing the divorce agreement with you?"

"She wasn't! I overheard her talking to Auntie Kelley."

I was relieved when Dad's face relaxed. Still, he closed his eyes for a long moment before speaking again. "Look, Jenna, she's right. It's not in the agreement, but I promise you, I'm paying for college. I don't need any legal document to enforce my responsibility to you as your dad. You can get scholarships if you want—you certainly are smart enough—but you don't need to worry about this."

"I don't understand." Why had Mom made such a big deal about it? "Maybe she didn't hear you or something?"

"She heard me. It's just the way your mom is. Too proud." Dad frowned. "She doesn't want my money. She thinks if I pay for things then somehow it makes her inferior. It's the thing we've fought about our entire marriage. But it has nothing to do with you. Trust me, Jenna. I've got college covered."

Just then our number boomed over the loudspeaker, and Dad got up to get our dinner. Emotions swirled in me, making me feel dizzy. Mom didn't want Dad to pay for my college. She wanted me to get scholarships and go into debt just to prove something to him. It was fine if she didn't want to take his money, but why couldn't I? I was his kid, too. And worse, why make me feel like Dad had bailed on me even more than I already did?

"Okay, wipe that frown off your face," Dad said, sitting down with our tray. "It's taco time!"

I smiled. He was right. I didn't want to waste this precious time with Dad being upset with Mom.

While we ate, Dad asked me about school. I caught him up on almost everything. But I didn't want to tell him about the scholarship. Even though he said he supported my getting scholarships, he'd probably just remind me that he'd come through for college, and it didn't matter if I won or lost. But I didn't only care about the prize money. I mean, I agreed with Mom. Independence was a good thing. It would be nice if I could fund part of my own college education. But I also wanted to prove that I had what it took to be a great reporter. And maybe, just maybe, that I was better than Elliot.

After dinner, we walked back to the car. "We still have some time," Dad said. "Want to take a walk on the pier?"

"Sure."

Dad drove the short distance to the pier parking lot, but he stopped me before I got out of the car. He reached into the back seat and handed me a brown paper bag.

"What's this?" I asked.

"I never did mail your gifts to you when I got back from Japan."

I opened the bag and pulled out two elegantly wrapped packages. I'd heard that in Japan every purchase was gift wrapped. I opened the flat package and found three reporter notepads with black leather covers. My heart leapt with joy.

"Oh, Dad! These are awesome!"

"I thought you'd like them. Open the other one!" he said, pointing to a narrow box.

I tore off the paper and flipped open the lid. Nestled inside was a fancy black-and-gold pen. I pulled it out and held it reverently.

"I got it engraved," Dad said.

I checked out the pen and found *Sakai* in Japanese.

"Dad! This must have been expensive."

He shook his head. "Not really. But it is a nice pen, so don't lose it or give it away."

"Ha!" As if I'd ever lost anything. And I would never give anything away Dad gave me. I still had the teddy bear and his *Hamilton* T-shirt that he didn't know about. "Thanks, Dad," I said. My heart squeezed so tight that I felt it in my throat. "I love these. They're perfect."

He smiled. "I'm glad you like them. Okay, let's go walk on the pier before I have to get you back home."

Just like that, the happiness I felt was washed away by sadness.

If only it were still Dad's home, too.

twenty-six

It took some doing, but by Thursday, I finally figured out where Rin's new pickup spot was.

I'd asked a few kids that I knew ate lunch in the music room and learned that Rin had a driver. Of course. Being rich and all. And if his parents worried about his safety enough to have him picked up, they probably wouldn't want him walking far from school to catch his ride. So far, I'd tried every spot that fit that description with no luck. There was only one place left to look: the parking lot of a burger joint across the street from the gym.

And my deductions paid off. The silver Lexus was

waiting there! But I'd already missed my chance. I watched Rin cross the street, approach the car, and slide inside.

It doesn't matter, I thought, smiling a secret smile. *No more waiting. Tomorrow I'm going to finally talk to him.*

The next day after school, the sky opened up just as the last bell rang. It hardly ever rained! And I hardly ever checked the weather. Fortunately, I had a rain jacket stuffed in my locker. I wrapped it around Rin's sketchbook and jogged across campus, keeping to the covered walkways until I got to the baseball field. I hugged the wrapped sketchbook to my chest and ran. My messenger bag and I got thoroughly soaked.

By the time I made it to the burger parking lot, my shoes squished and rain dripped from my hair as if I'd just gotten out of the shower. I spied Rin's car immediately and felt relieved I'd beaten him ... and hadn't gotten drenched for nothing.

I walked up to the driver's side, where a man with short blond hair sat reading a book propped up on the steering wheel. I knocked on the window, and he jumped, nearly dropping it. He was younger than I'd envisioned a driver. He looked like a college student. He smiled sheepishly and rolled the window down a crack.

"Hey," he said. "Everything okay?"

"Hi. I'm Jenna Sakai. I have something to return to Rin."

He nodded. "Oh yeah, I remember you."

Despite being wet with rain, I felt my ears burn. The only time he would have seen me was when I tried to return Rin's notebook the last time and he'd snubbed my offer, leaving me standing there looking stupid.

"I'm Tate." The driver unlocked the doors with a click. "Get in out of the rain while we wait for Rin. He should be here any minute."

"Thanks." I was pretty sure Mom would have a complete meltdown if she knew I was getting into a car with a man I didn't know, but if Rin's parents trusted Tate with their only son, then I was pretty sure I was okay. All the same, I kept my hand on the door handle and was relieved when Tate didn't lock it.

"So you're Rin's driver?" I asked.

Tate smiled. "That sounds fancy. I just take him where he needs to go after school since his parents are busy. It's a sweet gig and helps me pay for college."

The back door opened, and I got whacked by Rin's heavy, wet backpack. He climbed in after it, and when he saw me, his mouth dropped open. He glared. "What are *you* doing here?"

"I need to talk to you," I said.

"I don't want to talk to you. Get out of my car."

"It's pouring out there!"

"The weather is not my fault." Rin took in my dripping-wet-dog look. He was wearing a very nice rain jacket with an oversize hood that kept both his hair and glasses dry. "And you not having rain gear is also not my fault."

"I have a raincoat!"

"You're supposed to wear it!" Rin snapped.

I lifted my packet. "It's protecting your sketchbook!"

Rin stared at me.

Tate remained quiet in the front seat, neither starting the car nor reading his book. I could see in the rearview mirror his eyes ping-ponging between me and Rin. He didn't look alarmed. In fact, he looked amused.

"You got drenched because you were keeping my stupid sketchbook dry?" Rin asked. "I told you I didn't want it, especially if you're holding it hostage!"

"I'm not! And I'm not leaving!"

"Fine!" Rin grabbed his backpack. "Then I will!"

"Nope!" Tate finally spoke up. "That's not allowed, Rin, and you know it. Come on, man, don't make my job hard."

"Rin," I said. His name felt odd on my tongue. "Please. Can we go to the diner?"

"Fine." Rin put on his seat belt, and I did the same.

Tate started the car and pulled out of the parking lot.

"Sorry about getting the seat all wet," I said softly.

Rin blew out a breath and leaned over the back seat. He tossed a towel at me. "It's clean."

I wiped my face. The towel smelled like dryer sheets. I wrung out my hair and patted my clothes, but it was no use. They were drenched. I peeled off my sweatshirt. At least my T-shirt underneath was only damp. Rin grumbled under his breath and leaned back over the seat again. This time he tossed a jacket at me. I gratefully pulled it on. It was soft, fleecy, mint green, and not really Rin's style.

"It's my sister's," he said.

When we arrived at the diner a few short minutes later, the rain had tapered off to a misty drizzle.

Rin unbuckled his seat belt, grabbed his backpack, and flung open the door. I quickly followed him into the diner. I knew I could have given back his sketchbook in the car, but I had an apology to deliver. I dreaded having to say I was sorry and worried he'd refuse to accept it, but yet, here I was, back in the diner, feeling lighter than I had in days.

twenty-seven

"Jenna! Rin!" Leigh called out with glee, rushing over to us. "Welcome back, you two!"

Rin smiled as we dropped into our usual seats. A real smile.

"I've been worried," Leigh said to Rin. "Everything okay?"

"It's fine. Just got busy."

"The booth wasn't the same without you both. Rin, *Hamilton* shake for you and for Jenna the *Waitress* shake?"

"Sounds good," I said. "Thanks."

Rin and I were quiet as we waited for Leigh to return with our shakes. She sang a new song about how it only takes one taste to know something is good. It had to be from *Waitress* since I knew the entire *Hamilton* soundtrack.

Rin applauded, and I quickly joined in.

"On the house," Leigh said with a bow. "A welcome-back treat."

We sipped our shakes, and the silence drew out longer and longer.

"Why's it okay for Leigh to treat you, but not okay when I offer?" Rin asked suddenly.

That was none of his business. But I was here to try to apologize, and snapping at him wasn't a good way to start. "She's not trying to prove something. She's just being generous."

Rin raised his eyebrows. "And what am I trying to prove when I offer to treat?"

"That you're rich! And that the booth really belongs to you!" Oops. That came out before I could stop it.

"Wow, Sakai. You have issues."

We both got quiet again. I didn't know what it was about Rin that made me lose my cool. It was maddening. We both drank our shakes in silence.

Finally, I couldn't stand it anymore. I swallowed the last of my milkshake along with my pride.

"I'm sorry," I said.

Rin leaned back. "For?"

"For keeping your sketchbook."

Rin wiped his hands on his napkin, one finger at a time. He crumpled the paper and tossed it onto the table next to his empty shake glass. The longer he took to respond, the more annoyed I got. I clenched my hands into fists under the table and pressed them against my legs. I clamped my lips so that I wouldn't say anything I'd regret.

"That's it?" he said finally.

"What do you mean?"

"That was your apology? You're only sorry for keeping my book?"

"Yes. I mean I'm sorry for snapping at you, too."

Rin said nothing, but his eyes stayed on me.

"What?" I asked. If he was waiting for me to say more, he'd be sorely disappointed.

He shrugged, and I assumed that meant he accepted my apology. I unwrapped his sketchbook, leaving my wet rain jacket on the bench, and nudged it across the table to him.

Rin didn't reach for it, but I didn't miss how his eyes locked onto the cover.

"I told you I didn't want it back."

"Why not? It's really good."

"You looked at it?" His voice rose, but it sounded more like surprise than anger.

"You said you didn't want it."

"That didn't mean it was yours."

"What did you want me to do with it? Throw it away?"

He shrugged.

"Rin."

He startled, and I blushed. For some reason, saying his name felt too personal. I cleared my throat and tried again. If I said his name more often, maybe it wouldn't seem so strange.

"Rin, your drawings are really good."

"Thanks," he said, finally reaching for his sketchbook. He flipped through the pages backward. The fingers on his left hand twitched like he was itching to hold his pen and draw.

He paused when he got to the sketches he'd done of me in the diner. His eyes flit to me, and he looked embarrassed. But he kept turning pages until he found the drawing of his family dinner.

I moved over to him so that we were looking at it together. Our arms touched, and I drew back slightly, even though a part of me felt comforted by the contact. "I love this one," I said quietly. "You're lucky."

"Lucky?"

"Just that you have your whole family there at the dinner table."

Rin stared at me for so long that I squirmed. I'd revealed way more than I had intended with those few words. I wanted to smack myself for dropping my guard. It was time to pivot and get some answers.

"Does your sister come home to visit often? And does she help out with the family business at all? Do you?"

He shot me a simmering glare and slammed the book shut. I took the hint and moved back to my side of the booth. Once again, silence descended. It wasn't like we'd chatted away in the past, but this silence was different from all the others. It was full of unsaid things and pressed against me, heavy and dark. It made it hard to breathe.

I'd wanted to ask those questions, but I hadn't meant to ask them now. Not like that. So I tried something more neutral. "What other things do you like to draw?"

"I'll make you a deal," Rin said, his voice flatter than usual.

"Yeah?"

"We'll share the booth like before. No talking about personal stuff. No prying, no sharing, no questions. Okay?"

I blinked. That would have been the ideal situation when he'd first stolen my booth. No involvement, no conversation. But now? Now I wanted to know things.

Rin's hands were still and empty as he waited for my answer. They looked odd without a pen or pencil. I knew if I didn't agree that this would be it. He wouldn't show up here anymore.

And I'd miss . . . whatever this was.

Suddenly, I realized I wasn't here to get information from him for my article. I mean, yeah, I still hoped I could find the right facts I needed. But if I was being completely honest, I wanted to share this booth with Rin.

I took in the hard look on his face, the light missing from his eyes. He'd still show up here. But he didn't want us to be friends anymore. I could deal with that as long as I could see him.

I nodded and said, "Okay."

twenty-eight

Monday at the diner had been a little awkward, but we quickly fell back into our routine—comfortable silence sprinkled with occasional comments, but never anything personal. By Friday, I realized that I might have to accept that Rin and I weren't talking enough for me to get the information I needed to write my article. At least not in time for the deadline that was coming up in two weeks. Applying for the scholarship with a mediocre article I wasn't passionate about wasn't worth it. The thought of Elliot winning, and then gloating, set my teeth on edge.

But I could still beat him out for editor in chief of the

digital paper next year. And if Ms. Fontes decided on no editor in chief, I at least wanted to be a news or feature editor. I sighed. I'd have to turn something in to show I deserved it. I guessed writing the article highlighting the good things the donation had done for the school wasn't the worst thing in the world. But it wasn't going to win any contests. This whole situation stunk.

I watched Rin draw. At least he hadn't put up the textbook wall today. His long, tapered fingers gripped his pen as he moved it in sure strokes across the page. He was drawing a new manga character, and his glasses had slipped down to the tip of his nose. I waited. And as he always did, he pushed them back onto the bridge of his nose with his drawing hand. He never accidentally marked his face with his pen, even though he'd come close a few times. His hair fell across his forehead. It had gotten longer lately. Or maybe he'd stopped using so much product.

Suddenly, my phone rang. Both Rin and I jumped. I grabbed it and smiled when I saw who was calling.

"Dad! Hey, what's up?" I leaned back against the booth.

"Hey, kiddo! Where are you right now?"

"That diner I told you about. Why?"

"It's on Beach, right? I'm on my way."

"Wait." I bolted up. "You're here? In Pacific Vista?"

"Yep! Sit tight!"

I glanced at Rin, who had stopped drawing and was obviously listening to my end of the conversation.

"Dad, wait. I can meet you somewhere else. At school or even at my house."

"Nah, I'm almost there. See you in a minute!"

I ended the call and started packing my things.

"Your dad is coming to pick you up?"

I tossed my newspaper club notebook into my bag. Today, I'd doodled a lot.

"Does your dad not live with you?" Rin asked.

"Why would you assume that?" I scooped up my pens and dumped them into my pen case, but one of them rolled off the table and under the booth. I leaned down to snatch it up and then knocked my head against the table.

"Are you okay?" Rin asked. When I nodded, he continued. "You asked him if he was in Pacific Vista. And then you said you could meet him at *your* house, not *the* house."

Gah! Rin would probably make a better reporter than me. "I thought we had an agreement," I said as I scooted out of the booth, leaving money on the table for my bill. "No personal questions."

Rin tossed cash down, too, and grabbed his things.

"Why are you following me?" I asked as I waved good-bye to Leigh.

"I'm not. I'm leaving."

"Okay, then. Have a good weekend." I sat down on the vinyl bench at the door, relieved that Rin would be leaving first.

But no. Rin sat down next to me. "What are you doing?"

He grinned. "Sitting."

He was so annoying! "Why?"

"I think that's a personal question."

"You are not meeting my dad."

"Who said I wanted to meet your dad? Besides, you met Tate. In fact, you forced your way into the car." Rin's voice had a teasing note I'd never heard before. I wasn't sure I liked it. In fact, I was sure I didn't like it!

"Tate isn't your dad," I said.

Rin shrugged. "I see him more than I see either of my parents, so he might as well be."

"Oh?" I turned to him. "Why is that?"

Rin's face closed.

"See? You don't like talking about your family, either."

"I didn't ask you to talk about your family." Rin leaned back, stretching his legs out like he was going to be there for the long haul.

Fine! I stood up and left the diner. I'd wait outside. When Rin stepped out next to me, Tate, who was parked across the street, started the car, made a very illegal U-turn, and pulled up in front of us.

"See ya," I said.

Rin walked over to the Lexus. I relaxed. He would be long gone before Dad showed up. Rin tossed his backpack into the car, said something to Tate, who nodded, and then returned to stand next to me.

I ignored Rin. The more I made a big deal out of this, the more he seemed to get a kick out of tormenting me.

A few minutes later, I was surprised when Dad pulled up in a car that looked exactly like his blue BMW. Except it couldn't be since it was back in Texas.

"Nice wheels," Rin said.

"Shut up," I said. "It's a rental."

But when Dad parked in front of us, I saw it *was* his

car. I could tell by the tiny dent on the passenger side door from the time I'd accidentally bumped it with a shopping cart. Dad had been upset at first, but he said he knew it was an accident and told me to forget about it. Except I hadn't been able to because on the drive home Mom accused Dad of caring about the car more than he cared about me and they'd yelled at each other all the way home. In the end, I realized the fight had nothing to do with me or the dent, but it had still made me feel terrible.

As Dad shut off the engine, I was already reaching for the passenger door. Rin was faster and opened it for me. I gave him a death glare, but he ignored me and leaned down to look at my dad.

"Hi," he said. "I'm Rin."

Dad smiled. "Hello, Rin! Always happy to meet one of Jenna's friends."

My friend? That was a laugh. Friends talked to each other. About themselves and what was going on in their lives. Friends really knew each other!

"Do you need a ride?" Dad asked.

"No, he doesn't," I said, shoving Rin out of the way and getting in the car. "Goodbye." I yanked the door from his grip and closed it. He saluted before saunter-ing over to the Lexus.

"That wasn't very nice, Jenna," Dad said with a frown.

"Let's just go."

Dad raised his eyebrows at me. He started the car and pulled out into the street. I glanced back a few times to make sure Rin wasn't following us. This wasn't a spy movie. It was real life. *My* real life. I relaxed when the Lexus turned right at the first corner.

I faced Dad. "This is your car."

He smiled. "Yes, it is."

"Why do you have your car here?"

He laughed. A full-on Dad laugh.

"Dad!"

"Okay, okay, I'll tell you, but give me a few minutes."

Fine. I'd play his game and wait him out.

twenty-nine

Ten minutes later, we drove to a fancy condo complex halfway between the beach and school. Dad hit a button on his visor, and the metal gate in front of a parking garage rumbled open.

"What's going on?" I asked warily.

He pulled into a spot marked B-345 and got out of the car. I followed him through the garage to an elevator. My heart pounded as I added up the clues.

Dad and I rode up to the top floor, where an outdoor walkway overlooked the street. The sun beat down on my bare neck and sweat trickled down my back as Dad took out a set of keys and unlocked the door to B-345.

"Welcome home, kid."

I stepped into the foyer and looked around. The living room was bright with natural light streaming in from the big picture window that reflected on the white ceramic tile. In the distance, I could see a sliver of ocean. The faint hum of an air conditioner harmonized with the sounds of traffic outside.

Dad slipped off his shoes, and I did the same. Then he took my arm and tugged me into the living room. The couch and reading chair were dark brown leather, and sat next to a glass-topped coffee table and a wrought-iron standing lamp. Unlike his apartment in Texas, which was filled with ugly rental furniture, this room looked very much like Dad.

"What do you mean 'home'?" I asked.

"I've moved back!"

I blinked, looking around at the condo again. "Why didn't you tell me? What happened to your job in Texas? When did you get back? How long have you been here?" It had to have been long enough to find a place to live and furnish it. My voice squeaked higher with each question.

Dad's smile lost a few watts. "I wanted to surprise you. Is this not a happy surprise?"

"It's great, seriously. I'm definitely surprised." I took a breath. "Does Mom know?"

"She does."

I ran my hand along the buttery-soft leather of the couch. "How long will you be around?"

"I have no intention of leaving. I bought this condo." Dad sat down on the couch and patted the seat next to him. "I saw it a few months ago, and as soon as I knew for sure I was moving back, I was able to make a fast purchase."

"I don't understand. You were looking for a place here, but you didn't tell me?"

"Nothing was for sure, Jenna." Dad ran his hand through his salt-and-pepper hair. "I made a mistake."

Those were words I never thought I'd hear coming from Dad, or Mom for that matter.

"I thought the job in Texas would make me happy. It was a promotion, more money, and a new adventure."

I remembered overhearing those exact words just before he and Mom split up. Mom hadn't wanted to move. She'd also gotten a promotion at the accounting firm. In the end, Mom stayed, Dad left, and I had no say in any of it.

Dad leaned back against the couch. "The job wasn't nearly as interesting as I had hoped, and it turned out not to be an adventure, especially because I was alone. I missed you, kid."

I nodded. I didn't trust my voice, and my nose got sniffly.

"Anyway, I've been looking for something back in this area since before Thanksgiving. I got a job offer in January and accepted it. I was here last week to close on this condo." Dad smiled. "I went back to Texas to get my car and came back last weekend. New job started this week."

He'd been thinking about this since Thanksgiving? I'd spent all of Christmas break with him, and he hadn't said a word. And he'd moved back last weekend? Dad had been here for a whole week already and hadn't told me! I pressed my fists against my legs. I still hadn't talked to Mom about what Dad said about paying for college. All three of us kept everything locked inside. Why? Why didn't we talk about things that mattered?

When I didn't say anything, Dad cleared his throat and stood. "Let me give you the tour."

I followed him into a galley kitchen that shared a

nook with a small two-person table. From there we headed back through the living room down a short hall. My socks slid on the hardwood floors. There was a decent-size bathroom on the right. And he'd picked a king-size bed and plain dark blue comforter for the bedroom at the end of the hall.

Dad nudged me toward the other door in the hall, most likely his office. It was a small room with only one window, but the best view—the same sliver of sea as the living room. And it was totally empty.

"This is your room, Jenna. We can go shopping for furniture and stuff."

"What?" I turned to Dad.

"This is your bedroom. I talked to your mom, and you can spend as much time here as you'd like. We can be a family again."

The dam burst. "A family?" I said, my voice rising as the words flooded out of my mouth. "How can we be a family *again*? You and Mom are divorced! I have to split my time between two homes! How is that even close to being a family?"

"Jenna," Dad said, but I cut him off before he started spouting excuses.

"No! It's my turn!" I paced in circles around the room. "You and Mom made all these decisions that affected me and not once did either of you ask me what I wanted or what I thought! Not only that, but you never told me what was going on. Just like now! You make a decision that totally affects me, dump it on me, and expect me to be happy. Neither of you talk to me about anything important!"

Dad looked miserable. His whole body sagged, and he looked older than I'd ever seen him. But I didn't feel like cutting him a break. Not when he got everything he wanted, whenever he wanted! Like Mom said, money is power and Dad had plenty of it. Okay, so she hadn't said that to me, but I'd heard her on the phone. And now he thought a new bedroom was going to make me forgive all the secrets he'd been keeping?

"All you care about is money. You already make a lot, but you look for jobs that'll make you more. You spend it on things like fancy cars and"—I waved my hand around the condo—"fancy apartments with expensive furniture because you think those things will make you happy. But they won't. Money isn't more important than me!"

Dad's eyes were now wide in shock.

"You left me!" I yelled. "You left! You left!" I started sobbing and sank down onto the hard cold floor.

I expected Dad to get all uncomfortable and leave the room. To "give me space." Instead, I felt his arms wrap around me tightly. I cried into his shoulder like I was four years old and had skinned my knee.

Except this time it was my heart that had peeled wide open.

Thirty

After my tears had dried, I pulled away and scooted back against the wall, swiping my sleeve against my snotty nose and rubbing my eyes on my shoulder. Dad left the room and returned with a roll of toilet paper for me. I ripped off a long piece and blew my nose.

Dad sat down across from me. "Well," he said, his voice a little shaky. "I don't know what to say. Except I'm sorry. I don't think either your mother or I realized how much all this affected you." He blew out a big breath. "I mean, of course, it affected you."

I sighed.

"I'm not very good at talking about things," Dad

said, looking down at the floor. "I think that was probably part of the problem between your mom and me. Neither of us were good at expressing our true feelings. Resentments build when you can't talk about what's bothering you."

That was for sure. I clutched the roll of toilet paper to my chest, still trembling from my unexpected outburst.

"I get that you felt out of the loop," Dad continued, "but the decisions we fought over were between your mom and me. They had nothing to do with you. You were never the problem." He shook his head when he caught my look.

"The thing you say about money is only partly true. Yes, I make good money and I like the comfort it brings me. Us. That money pays for your lifestyle, Jenna, whether or not you appreciate it. The nice home, your clothes, all the books, and a generous allowance that lets you do things with your friends. It's also going to pay for your college education. You can study whatever you want. So, let me be clear, yes, money is nice, but I would never choose it over you.

"I didn't leave *you*, Jenna. I know it felt like it, but I didn't. You were always on my mind. And you are the reason I came back. You are the only reason I came back."

I wanted to believe him. To believe he was back for good. At the same time, I didn't trust that things would be different. Mom was still Mom. Dad was still Dad. I'd been angry with both of them, but I realized that while I'd been frustrated with Mom for being so mean about Dad and refusing to talk to me about him, I mostly blamed Dad for the divorce. I'd felt completely abandoned. I gave Mom more of a break because he'd left her, too. She'd stayed.

But Mom was just as much to blame. She'd pushed Dad away and refused help because somehow she saw it as a weakness. She was stubborn and proud. Guess I knew where I got that from.

"Jenna, here." Dad came over to me and ripped off more toilet paper. I hadn't realized I'd started crying again.

"Keeping things from you didn't help," Dad said. "I see now that I wasn't protecting you; I was protecting myself. That was selfish. I'm sorry."

I nodded. In the silence that followed, I wondered if I would ever be able to talk like this with Mom. She was even harder to talk to than Dad.

I was ready for this conversation to be over. I glanced

around the small room, trying to absorb that this would be mine. "Mom's okay with this? With me spending time here?" I couldn't believe they could have a civil conversation about anything, much less this.

Dad sighed quietly. "We're working it out. However much time you want to spend here, or not, is fine with both of us. Your mom would like you to create some sort of schedule so we know where you are and when, but there's no rush. We can play it by ear for now."

"Okay."

"Do you feel like going shopping?" Dad asked, rubbing his chin. "At the very least we should get you a bed and some linens."

I nodded. "That sounds good."

~

The rest of the weekend was a whirlwind of shopping with Dad. Mom was working, and it had been nice to have Dad around after all. Or maybe Mom chose to work so she wouldn't have to miss me. We didn't discuss it, which meant I'd probably never know.

Keiko met me at home on Sunday evening. "So," she said as we settled in my room. "Are you happy your dad is back?"

"It's complicated." It felt good to talk about my dad. The one person I could always count on was Keiko, and I didn't want to keep my feelings in anymore. I told her about my conversation with my dad, and that I'd cried. About how frustrated I was with both my parents for keeping things from me. I even told her about how my digging into the cafeteria renovation hadn't led to anything and that the donation might not be an evil plot after all.

The whole time, Keiko just listened, letting me talk and talk until I was talked out.

In the silence that followed, I wondered if I'd said too much.

Keiko picked up my teddy bear and sat him on her lap. "I'm glad you got everything off your chest with your dad," Keiko said finally.

"That's it?" I asked. "No other questions?"

"I'm sorry I've been so pushy. I know you hate it when people pry into your life. It's only because I care about you."

I reached over and took my teddy bear and hugged him to me. "No, I'm the one who's sorry. I don't know why I was so grouchy with you."

Keiko laughed. "I do."

I gave her the side-eye.

"You don't like talking about your feelings," she said. "I get it."

"But maybe keeping them locked up isn't good for me."

"Agreed." Keiko poked my leg. "Have you talked with your mom?"

"No. I feel like she's avoiding me on purpose."

"Why are moms so hard to talk to?" Keiko asked. She'd gotten into a huge fight with her mom a few months ago.

"But things are better between both of you now, right?"

She smiled. "Much."

Then there was hope.

"How's your scholarship application going?" Keiko asked. "I can't wait till you're done and we can hang out again."

I groaned.

"What's up?" she asked.

"Maybe I'm not cut out to be a reporter," I said.

"Why would you say that?"

"My article isn't working."

"What do you mean?"

"I need hard-hitting facts. Something noteworthy."

"Jenna," Keiko said in that tone of hers. "Didn't you just say that everything you learned showed that the donation was aboveboard? The foundation helps feed hungry kids. That's a good thing!"

"Yeah, but it doesn't make for an interesting article. I'm supposed to be exposing truths."

"The donation is legit. Isn't that the truth?"

"It's *a* truth. But I have a gut feeling there's more to the story." Although I realized it was more a wish than a gut feeling. It was hard to let go of hope.

"Okay, fine. If you want to know the real deal, why can't you ask Rin?"

"Trust me, I can't." I told her about our no-personal-conversation arrangement.

Keiko shook her head. "I can't believe it. You found the guy version of you."

"What are you talking about?"

"Rin is just like you. He doesn't like to talk about things."

"I talk about things!" I took a breath. Actually, no, I didn't. Until now. The last couple of days had made me feel lighter. Even though talking about my feelings didn't change what happened, it made me feel unburdened. Like Dad and Keiko were helping to carry the load a little.

"I mean, I know I have a hard time with it, but I'm starting to realize that keeping everything locked up is tiring. I don't want that anymore."

Keiko nodded. "So, what *do* you want?"

I squeezed my plush bear. "It's too much. I want too much." I wanted my parents to get back together or at least never fight. I wanted to write the winning scholarship entry for PV Middle. I wanted ... dreams that felt so big I couldn't even name them.

"Well, one thing's for sure, you won't have to go away to Texas this summer." Keiko grinned.

I smiled back at her. I'd been so lost in my head about how much I hated surprise changes and not being told what was going on that I forgot to focus on the good stuff.

"You're one of the strongest and smartest people I know," Keiko said. "Whatever you want, go for it."

She was right. I could figure it all out. Maybe I could make some of my dreams come true.

Even the big ones.

thirty-one

On Monday, Elliot was waiting for me at my locker after school. He wore his favorite jacket, the one with lots of pockets so he could keep a notebook and pen on him at all times.

"Hey," he said.

"What are you doing here?" I asked.

"Can we talk?"

I waved my hand between us. "We're talking."

"I meant, alone, somewhere."

"We *are* alone. And we have newspaper club in five minutes."

"I have some information for you, for that article

you're writing about the cafeteria renovation."

I crossed my arms. "How do you know what I'm working on?"

He smiled and shrugged. It wasn't nearly as cute as when Rin did it. Like everything else about him, Elliot's shrug seemed patronizing.

"Seriously, Elliot!"

"What? I'm an excellent investigative reporter."

"You're a sneak," I said.

"Whatever. Do you want the information or not?"

I wanted to tell him to get lost, but I was curious. Reporters didn't walk away from sources.

"Okay. Spill it," I said as I opened my locker.

"The money came from a foundation," he said.

"Yeah, I know."

He went on. "I also found out not all the donation was used for the cafeteria renovation."

"Oh, Elliot." He didn't know as much as I did; that was clear. I grabbed my math book and turned to walk away.

"Wait, Jenna! I have more," he said.

I took a deep breath and turned back around.

"I got a hold of the construction records, and it came

in under a million. We need to find out where the other part of the donation went!"

"We?"

"I mean, you."

I already knew where that money went. It had funded the new kitchen staff and supplemented the free lunch program. But there was no way I was telling Elliot that. "Look, I don't need your help."

"The foundation is in trouble."

"What do you mean?"

Elliot flashed a triumphant grin. "The couple who founded Feed Schools is having marriage trouble."

Rin's parents? "That's just gossip. And it has nothing to do with the renovation."

"No? It turns out that the donation wasn't approved by the foundation. The wife did it all on her own, even though she was supposed to get approval from the foundation itself."

I rolled my eyes. Traci Watanabe *was* the foundation. She didn't need to get approval from herself. And how sexist of Elliot to assume that she needed permission! Elliot had nothing.

Still, he kept talking. "Her husband didn't know what

she'd done until after the money had been donated. He tried to get it back, and there was a huge stink."

I paused. Had Rin's dad tried to control the foundation's spending? According to their website, he didn't have anything to do with it. Interference like this could be what I needed to get my article on track. But instead of the rush of excitement I expected, I felt something more like regret. The thought that maybe Rin might be feeling like I had when my parents got divorced filled me with sadness.

"Come on, you know as well as I that something shady is probably going on," said Elliot. "Don't you want to investigate it?"

"Why are you doing this?" I asked. "Why are you trying to help me?"

"I said it before, Jenna. We make a great team."

I said nothing.

"Well, we used to be a great team," Elliot amended.

"No. We weren't."

"Don't be like that, Jenna."

"I'm not being like anything. You always try to make me feel bad for wanting credit for my ideas."

"Oh my God, Jenna! Are you going to start that again?"

I blinked at him. "You seriously don't see it. You don't think you've ever stolen my work at all?"

"We were writing those articles together!"

Arguing with him wasn't worth it. In fact, this reminded me of my parents. They'd get in the same fights over and over, never coming to any agreement or compromise. It had been miserable to listen to, and it wasn't fun being in the thick of it, either. I couldn't change Elliot. I had zero control over what he did or thought or said. I only had control over my own actions.

"Where did you find out about the Watanabes?" I asked.

"I'll tell you if you let me work on the story with you."

"Forget it! This is *my* entry for the scholarship!"

"We can probably submit it together. Split the prize!"

"What happened to the great article you were working on?"

Elliot played with the zipper on his jacket. "It didn't pan out."

He wasn't perfect after all. And now he was trying to glom onto my work. Again. "No way," I said. "I'm the one who came up with the idea. I'm the one whose been researching all along."

"But you didn't know anything about the Watanabes' marriage until I told you."

"Where did you find that out anyway?"

"Agree to work with me first."

I studied Elliot. For once, he didn't look so smug. He looked worried. Which meant I had a real chance to win that scholarship.

But how badly did I want it? Right now my article was nowhere, and if Elliot knew something that could make it the kind of impressive exposé I'd originally wanted to write, I was sure to be chosen to represent PV Middle in the competition. But anything he knew about Rin's parents' marriage could only be speculation. And what kind of story would that make? It wasn't news, just gossip. And it would hurt Rin. No. Even if it made my article more exciting, I didn't want to win anything that way.

"Admit you need me," Elliot said. "You can't write that article without me."

"Watch me." I turned to leave, but Elliot grabbed on to my messenger bag.

"Jenna, wait! I take it back! Breaking up, I mean. I want to get back together."

My brain went blank.

"We're the same," Elliot said, still holding on to the strap of my bag. "We made each other better." He actually seemed sincere. But it didn't matter. I wasn't interested. Not anymore.

I glared at him, and he dropped his hand. "You don't want to get back together," I said. "You want to work on the winning article." My hands started to ache, I was clenching them so tightly.

Why couldn't he just leave me alone? I'd stopped talking to him, avoided him as much as possible, and been totally unfriendly so he would keep away. I'd even gotten rid of everything that reminded me of Elliot so I could pretend he'd never existed.

I paused, and my ears got hot as I made a connection. My mom tried to erase all evidence of Dad just like I was trying to do with Elliot. I thought Mom hated Dad and had never cared about him at all. But that probably wasn't it. Mom was hurting.

Burying memories didn't make the pain go away at all.

"Jenna?" Elliot broke into my thoughts.

"No, Elliot. I don't want to get back together. We may

have the same goals, but we're not the same when it comes to things that really matter."

Elliot and I had always said it was important to be objective, no matter what we were talking about. And I always thought I was pretty good at it. But really, I'd just been closed off. To my feelings, and to other people. I judged everyone without knowing the truth or the facts. All that anger I felt about the donation was about how money made me feel, and all that anger I had about money was really about my parents. I hadn't been objective at all.

Elliot wasn't as objective as he thought, either. He didn't think he'd taken credit for my work. And maybe he really believed that. But he wasn't my problem anymore.

Elliot's eye grew wide. "You seriously don't want to know what I found out about the Watanabes?"

"Nope." I'd been wrong about so many things, but I was sure about this. "And don't even think about trying to write about the donation with your spin. Ms. Fontes has seen a draft of my story already. We've discussed it. And if you try to turn in something similar, she'll know you stole it!" I dug around in my bag, grabbing Elliot's pen. "Here," I said, handing it to him. "It's your favorite, right?"

"I gave that to you. You can keep it."

I shook my head. "I have my own." The one Dad gave me was the only one I'd be using for my newspaper articles.

"Fine." Elliot shoved the pen into one of his pockets. "What about the article?"

"You're not writing it," I said to Elliot. "I am."

"Oh, come on, Jenna! Be a team player for once!"

I walked away. I *would* be a team player, but I was going to choose who was on my team.

Thirty-two

After newspaper club—where Elliot and I totally ignored each other—I went straight to the diner. When I saw the booth was empty, my heart fell.

Where was Rin? I'd been super rude to him when Dad had picked me up. But not ruder than any other time. Keiko said I pushed people away. Had I pushed Rin too hard this time? We'd always bickered but in a good-natured way. But maybe Rin didn't think so. Maybe he was fed up with me.

I looked at the menu wondering if I should try something new. But really all I wanted was my *Waitress* strawberry milkshake and to share cheesy Fetch Fries with

Rin. When had I stopped coming here to be alone and started coming to share the booth with Rin?

"Why so glum? No good specials?" Rin asked as he sat down across from me.

I couldn't stop the smile spreading across my face. "Hi! Where were you?"

Rin raised his eyebrows at me. "Um. Hi? And helping Tom again."

Leigh strode up to our booth and placed matching shakes in front of us. "I'm trying something new and combining your favorites. I'm calling it We Go Together like Strawberry and Chocolate. From *Grease*."

My ears warmed. For once, Leigh didn't sing and slipped away as quickly as she'd arrived. I took a long sip and felt my shoulders loosen. This new shake was really good. The combination of our favorite flavors was rich and sweet, with a sharp tartness at the end that I found irresistible. I glanced at Rin. As he sipped his shake, his glasses slipped down his nose. I waited, and moments later, he pushed them back up, the gesture as familiar as the guarded look on his face. I took another gulp of my shake, and when I looked back at Rin, our eyes met and my heart sped up.

"I'm sorry," I said, pushing the words out in a rush. "I shouldn't have snapped at you when I found out that your parents made the donation. I shouldn't have judged at all. And I'm sorry for being so rude. And for looking at your sketchbook."

Rin turned his milkshake glass in his hands, spinning it in slow circles. "You already apologized for all that."

"I know. I meant it before, but I *really* mean it now."

I'd thought about it the whole walk over to the diner. Yes, I wanted to enter the scholarship competition. Yes, I wanted to be an editor on the paper next year. Yes, I wanted to be a great reporter. But telling the truth was more important than an award, or money, or even beating Elliot. And so was Rin.

I pushed on. "I want you to know I'm not writing that article anymore. There won't be an exposé because there's nothing to expose."

"Just so you know," Rin said, "I didn't realize my mom had funded the cafeteria renovation. It's not like she runs things by me."

I shook my head. "You don't need to explain anything to me. It's none of my business."

"I thought you wanted to be a big-time investigative reporter."

"I do. The good kind."

"What's the good kind?"

"Objective. Looks for facts without judgment. And follows through on assignments."

Rin shrugged. Of course. He dug into his backpack to get his sketchbook and something to draw with.

"Pencil?" I asked. "No black felt-tip pen today?"

He raised his eyebrows. "That's a personal question."

I played with the straw in my glass, swirling it around the thick shake. The thing was, I wanted to get to know Rin better. And I wanted him to get to know me, too.

"If you're drawing with pencil," I said slowly, "that means you're either working on a realistic drawing or sketching a new manga character."

Rin stared at me for a long beat. I couldn't tell if I'd upset or annoyed him. But then he smiled. Not one of his arrogant full-on grins but a small smile. A private one.

He returned to drawing, and I watched his pencil move in long smooth strokes. In moments, a face formed. It amazed me that a pencil could render something so real looking. Soon the face became more detailed with high cheekbones, slightly narrowed eyes, and thick eyebrows pulled toward the middle in something like a scowl. A button nose. A mouth with full lips set in a straight line.

"Hey!" I exclaimed.

Rin's pencil stilled, and he looked up at me, that cocky grin back on his face. "Is there a problem?"

I scowled and then quickly rearranged my features to look less angry. "Is that how I look?"

Rin glanced down at his drawing. "Most of the time. Yeah."

That made me frown again. But I didn't want to be angry anymore. I'd been angry for years. I was tired. Pushing people away was exhausting. And lonesome.

Rin put his pencil down and leaned back, studying me for so long that I suddenly became very interested in my milkshake. I stirred and sipped and stirred again, staring down at the chocolaty liquid.

"I'll trade you one for one," I said without letting myself think too hard about what I was offering.

"What do you mean?"

"You get one personal question, but I get one, too." I

looked up at Rin, worried he'd shut me down, but he looked contemplative.

After a few more long seconds of silence, Rin said, "Okay. You get one question, so make it good."

"Who goes first?" I asked, suddenly nervous.

"Jan-ken-pon?" Rin asked.

I smiled. I put out my fist, and at the same time, we chanted, "Jan, ken, pon!" I opened my hand for my lucky sign, paper.

Unfortunately, Rin flashed his two fingers into scissors. "I win," he said with a little too much glee.

I crossed my arms. "Fine. Go."

"What's up with your parents?"

Wow. He didn't pull punches. "What do you mean?" I asked.

"Quit stalling, Sakai. We made a deal."

"They're divorced."

"And?"

"You asked a question. I answered."

He shrugged. "Fine. Then my answer to your question will be equally vague."

I took a long sip of my milkshake until the straw made a horrible slurping sound. I'd hit bottom. Rin waited.

"My parents fought all the time when they were married. I mean, *all* the time. At first, I tried to fix things. I thought if I was super good, did well at school, never asked for anything, stayed quiet, they wouldn't have anything to argue about. But it didn't help. I started hiding in my room and staying out of the way to avoid having to hear them." I sighed. "It wasn't always like that. We used to be a happy family. A team. But somewhere along the way, they stopped playing on the same side, and then they split up. My dad moved to Texas and now my mom never says anything nice about him."

I looked up at Rin, who was listening quietly. I wondered if I'd made him think of his parents.

"Up until recently I thought that if I'd been a better daughter my dad would have stayed," I continued. "So, when my dad showed up here and told me he was moving back, you'd think I would have been overjoyed."

"You weren't?" Rin asked.

"Not at first. I'd been so angry at him for leaving, and it all came out in a flood. Which was horrifying but also good because my dad and I finally talked. I'd been making assumptions about a lot of things, not only about my parents. I hate being wrong."

Rin nodded. "Yeah. Nobody likes to be wrong."

We sat in silence. I had no idea what Rin was thinking, but I wasn't sorry I'd told him all that. I wasn't embarrassed by anything I said. I wondered what that meant.

"Your turn," he said.

thirty-three

"Why aren't you in the art program?" I asked.

Rin scowled. "That's your question? You realize you only get one..."

"I know."

"Aren't you going to ask me about my parents' corporation? Or how much money they make?" Rin asked quietly.

"I told you, I'm not doing that article anymore," I said, matching his gentle tone. "And I thought it was my turn to ask a question."

"AkiWata Corporation is hugely successful," Rin said. "My grandpa put together his own company and factory with a loan from a family friend."

"Rin," I said in a warning tone.

He waved his hand. "I'm answering your question."

"The one I actually asked?"

"The one you actually asked."

"Okay, fine, but get to the part about you. I already found out about your family's business online."

Rin raised his eyebrows at me, and I blushed, realizing what I had just admitted.

"You didn't find all of this," he promised. "When my dad got married, Grandpa handed the company over to him. Grandpa had been grooming my dad for that since he was born. But even though my parents run the company together and my mom has her MBA and helped make it even more successful, Mom never got an official title. My grandpa is kind of traditional . . . in other words, sexist. But Mom wanted something of her own, so she started the Feed Schools Foundation. She's always been passionate about ending hunger for kids and providing good nutrition. And she's made Feed Schools as big a success as AkiWata."

"That's pretty impressive," I admitted. "But what does it have to do with you and art?"

"My sister, Sarah, wants to work at the corporation

when she's done with college and business school. She's determined to prove herself to Grandpa."

"Oh," I said. "She wants to take over eventually?"

Rin nodded. "But Grandpa wants it handed down from father to son. He's super old-fashioned."

"And wrong."

"You won't get me to argue that."

A light bulb went off in my head. "Your grandfather expects *you* to run the company. He won't support you pursuing art as a career."

Rin shrugged and folded his hands on the table. "My dad agrees with Grandpa. They both want me to take over."

"But you're in seventh grade!" I jiggled my legs. "How can they put that kind of pressure on you? You should have a say in what you do with your life. Have you told your parents you don't want to do it?"

"I don't want to disappoint them."

"Rin!" I threw my hands up.

"Sarah's plan is to change their minds. She's going to finish college before I even have to apply. I have time."

"You do," I said. "I mean, you don't have to make up your mind about your future now, but you should be able to be an artist if you want to. You should at least be able to take art classes."

Rin shook his head. "You don't understand."

"You have to speak up, tell your parents how you feel. I mean, it's a lesson I'm just now learning. I still have to talk to my mom about all the things she's been hiding from me."

"Then you know how hard it is," Rin said. "Why bother? It won't make a difference."

"It might. Maybe not right away, but over time." I was careful with my next question. "Are your parents okay?"

"What do you mean?"

"Are they happy together?"

Rin frowned. "Why are you asking that?"

I thought better of revealing my source. "You said you didn't want to disappoint them. It reminded me of how hard I tried to be the perfect daughter when my parents weren't getting along. I thought that might stop them from fighting so much."

"They're fine."

"That's good to hear."

I hesitated a moment and then said, "So that drawing you did of your family in your sketchbook?"

Rin gave me a long look. "Whatever you might have read about them is wrong. My parents might have been disagreeing about some stuff, but everything is better. Or getting better. That sketch was the first dinner we'd had together as a family that felt normal again."

"Why didn't you want the sketchbook back, then?"

"I think that's a second question."

"You're right. I guess I can fill in the blanks on my own."

Rin huffed. "Fine. I didn't want it back because I was mad at you, and half those drawings were of you."

Oh. "But we're good now?"

"We will be when you're done interrogating me." He said that with a light tone at least. Then he pointed to the menu. "Want to try something new?"

Huh. Great minds think alike. I nodded, and he waved me over so we could look at the menu together, even though there were no less than four of them propped against the napkin holder. I scooted until we sat side by side. My arm tingled even though we weren't touching.

We decided to share the *Waitress* Deep Dish Blueberry Bacon Pie. As we ate, we talked about his science quiz, and I convinced him to stop by the bake sale on Monday.

And he told me about his next open mic performance in two weeks.

"Your friend Isabella is going," Rin said. "For the article she's writing."

"Cool."

"Are you going to come?"

"Maybe."

He shrugged. "I want you to be there."

I stabbed a blueberry with my fork, feeling my ears burn. "Oh. Well, then okay. I'll be there."

When we were done eating, I accepted Rin's offer of a ride to my dad's condo. Mom was working late. I texted Keiko on the way so she could have her mom drop her off. When I got to my dad's, she was waiting for me.

"This is awesome, Jenna!" Keiko crossed into my new room.

Dad was the king of rush deliveries. Now I knew how he'd gotten all his furniture so quickly. He and I had spent most of Sunday night putting everything together just right.

I was still getting used to it. Keiko looked left and right, her smile as bright as the yellow sunflower quilt on my IKEA bed. Putting that together had nearly undone the truce between Dad and me.

"Go ahead and say it," I prompted.

Keiko looked around my room once more. I followed her gaze as she took in the framed art on my walls. One was of all the characters from Studio Ghibli movies, not unexpected. The other was a mossy-green watercolor with bare trees. It would have been a dark emo scene— the kind that was normally my style—but the branches were dotted with bright glowing circles that reminded me of fairy lights. Very unlike me. When I'd seen it at the art market Dad and I had gone to at the pier, I couldn't stop gaping at it. He'd bought it for me without a word.

Keiko walked over to my desk. Instead of textbooks or newspapers, there was a new sketchbook, very similar to the one Rin used, and a case of markers.

"What are you expecting me to say?" Keiko asked, sitting down on my bed again.

"That this room doesn't look like me." I leaned against my desk, facing her.

"It looks like you, Jenna."

"It does?"

Keiko smiled. "If you're looking for a fight, you've got the wrong person. I love this room." She held up her hand. "And I love your room at the house, too. They're both you."

"Really?"

"Really." Keiko patted the quilt. "Sunflowers are your favorite. You always comment on them whenever we see any. And you love Miyazaki films. We both do. That tree print is very cool. And your desk is stacked with art supplies. I've seen you drawing more than usual, but you've *always* drawn in your notebooks and handmade cards for my birthday."

She smiled at me, and I relaxed. I sat at my desk and opened my sketchbook where I'd already doodled a few new food characters. A piece of pie and a milkshake. I turned to a fresh page in my sketchbook, uncapped my pen, and drew a french fry. Then I drew eyes, a nose, a mouth, and stick arms and legs. Keiko peered over my shoulder.

"Cute," she said. "But the bubble tea one is still my favorite."

It was strange to do something for fun. I didn't dream of becoming an artist. I still wanted to be a writer. But I didn't feel like I had to only do things that moved me toward a goal anymore.

Keiko's phone dinged with a text from Conner. She smiled and sat down on my bed to chat with him. As her thumbs flew, her smile grew. I loved seeing her happy. And I loved her. I was so grateful that after years of me holding her at arm's length, of me being snappish and standoffish, she never ever gave up on me.

In fact, I felt lighter than I had in forever. Dad hadn't left because he wanted to get away from me, or even from Mom. And he'd returned. I knew he and mom would never get back together. I was pretty sure that was for the best—I didn't miss the fights and the yelling and the anxiety and resentment. For the first time in a long time, I was actually letting myself feel happy. Letting myself feel.

Keiko laughed at something Conner texted. She looked up at me. "Sorry! I'm almost done."

"No rush," I said.

My thoughts flitted to Rin. I didn't know when it happened, but I looked forward to spending time with him. I could totally be myself with him. At first that was because I didn't care what he thought, but eventually, I did care and nothing changed. He didn't judge me for being moody or smart or... anything. Wow. Maybe I liked him a little more than I thought I did.

"OMG, Jenna," Keiko squealed. "You are totally blushing! What are you thinking about?"

She dropped her phone and scurried to my desk.

"You know."

"Rin?"

"Rin."

"Jenna!" Keiko laughed and gently punched my arm.

It was still hard to talk about my feelings. That was going to take practice. Luckily, I was very good at putting in the work. And I had an idea for my first self-imposed assignment, which I couldn't wait to tell Keiko about.

"I think I know what I'm going to write about for the scholarship."

Thirty-four

The rest of the week flew by. I was back to hanging out with Keiko on Tuesdays and Thursdays, and it felt good. Rin and I spent our time at the diner, but even though we'd shared some deep thoughts, I stayed true to our deal. After those two personal questions, we went back to our usual routine. Bantering, eating, doing homework (me), and drawing (him). Mom was working a lot of late hours, so I spent evenings with Dad. I'd hardly seen her at all since he'd moved back. It was almost as if she were avoiding me.

On Sunday, I went to Dad's for a reinstated curry night. We cooked together, chopping onions, potatoes, and carrots. Dad browned the chicken pieces. I broke the blocks of chocolate-brown curry into pieces before dropping them into the bubbling mixture. The smell of spices filled the small kitchen and mingled with the starchy scent of rice steaming in the rice cooker.

"I spoke to your mom," Dad said as we sat down to eat.

"About?"

"A lot of things, but mostly about you. I'm afraid that your mom and I haven't modeled good behavior, particularly when it comes to talking about things. We are both ashamed that we hadn't realized how hurt you were. We should have known, of course, but you seemed to take it all so well. But I see now that your silence meant quite the opposite."

I scooped a spoonful of curry into my mouth.

"We both want you to know that the divorce didn't happen because of anything you did or said. It was all us. And we don't love you any less than we did before."

I swallowed. "But you don't love each other anymore."

Dad put down his chopsticks and nodded solemnly. "That is mostly true. I think deep down we will always care about each other, but the wounds are still fresh. It may take us a while to recover. And maybe someday we will be friends."

I raised my eyebrows, and Dad chuckled. "Yeah, hard to believe, but you can't predict the future. What you can do is try to create the circumstances for the kind of future you want. That's what I'm trying to do, Jenna. I'm here. And I'm not going anywhere. Okay?"

"Okay," I said.

We finished eating dinner while we talked about plans for the weekend. Dad's new job didn't require much travel, so that meant more free time, something he hadn't had much of at his other job. Once tax season was over, I would be able to spend more weekends with Mom. We were all still working out the living arrangements, but I could see switching it up in the summer—spending the week at Dad's and the weekends at Mom's. The thought of not having to be apart from either parent for weeks at a time lifted a huge weight off my chest. Maybe things were getting better after all.

When I got home, Mom was watching TV.

"Hi, Jenna," Mom said, holding up a bowl of popcorn. "Join me?"

I kicked off my shoes and went to sit next to her.

"You doing okay? With Dad?"

"Yeah." I grabbed a handful of popcorn and munched. I begged silently in my head, *Please don't say anything about Dad*, but I knew it was useless. Mom could never let an opportunity to bash him slip by.

Mom patted my leg. "Do you have time for a movie?"

I blinked at her. "Sure."

"Your choice. Anything you want." Mom handed me the remote.

"Okay." I clicked on the menu and scrolled to Miyazaki's *Spirited Away*. That had been one of Dad's favorites. I knew I was testing Mom, but I couldn't help it. "This one okay?"

"Hmmm," Mom said. "One request."

Here we go. "What?"

"We watch it in Japanese with English subtitles. Is that okay?"

I blinked at her again. "Okay."

Maybe what Dad said was true. Maybe they both really were going to work on being more aware of my feelings. Mom and I settled back against the couch, each of us wrapped in our blankets, and watched the movie together.

Thirty-five

On Monday, at newspaper club, I joined Isabella and Caitlin at our table. My stomach was in knots because I wanted to ask each of them a favor.

I hated asking favors. But I'd finally figured out I couldn't do everything alone.

"How's your scholarship entry going?" Isabella asked me.

"Okay." I still wasn't ready to talk about it. "Are you applying?"

"Actually, I think I am."

"That's awesome!"

"You don't mind a little competition?" Isabella nudged my arm.

"Bring it on," I said.

We smiled at each other.

"Hey, can I get a ride with you to open mic next week?" I felt awkward, like I was forcing myself into her free time.

"You want to go again?"

I nodded.

"That'd be great! None of my friends want to go," she said. "I mean, except for you."

"We're friends?"

"Jenna, you are hilarious!"

Happiness bubbled up in me. Knowing that Isabella felt the same as I did about our growing friendship gave me the confidence to ask the next thing. I turned to Caitlin. "Remember when you mentioned doing a cartoon with food characters?"

Caitlin nodded. "Does this mean you want to do one with me?"

"Maybe just one? To see how it goes?" I was doodling every day and was having a blast.

"You got it!" Caitlin said.

As I pulled out my newspaper club notebook, I felt warm inside. I glanced across the room at Elliot, who looked up just as my eyes landed on him. I nodded and turned back around in my seat to face my friends. No matter what happened with the scholarship or whatever assignments Ms. Fontes handed out next year, I belonged here.

～

On Tuesday, after telling Keiko what I was up to and knowing she'd be more than fine with me skipping out on the guys' basketball game, I made my way to the burger joint's parking lot.

"Hey, Tate," I said.

He smiled at me through the open window. It was finally getting warm, and flowers were blooming everywhere. Mom's allergies were totally acting up.

"Waiting for Rin?" Tate asked.

I nodded just as I saw Rin crossing the street toward the parking lot. I started walking toward him. My heart did a weird skipping thing.

"Sakai," he said when he reached me.

"Rin."

We stood on the corner, the current of students

flowing around us to get burgers after school. If they only knew about Leigh's diner, they wouldn't settle for mediocre fries.

"I want to renegotiate our terms," I said.

"Do you now?"

"Yep. I want to ask personal questions, and I want you to answer. And I want you to ask me questions."

"Cool." Rin started walking, and I followed. When we got to the car, Rin opened the back door and waved me in.

"So," I said to clarify, "I can ask you anything I want to?"

"Like I could stop you," he said with a grin.

When we got to the diner, Leigh brought us our chocolate-strawberry shakes and cheesy fries; then Rin took out his sketchbook and I took out mine. Our eyes met, and I could tell he wanted to ask me something. I shrugged a very Rin-like shrug.

"They're just doodles," I said.

"Can I see?"

I passed the slim sketchbook to him. I was nervous about showing him my drawings but not because I thought he'd make fun or be critical. I knew he wouldn't. I trusted him. But deep down, I wanted him to like them.

He flipped the book open and found my bubble tea character. On the next page was the pat of butter dancing with a toast. I stopped looking at the pages and instead watched Rin's face. His eyes scanned each drawing, and a smile played on his lips. Not like he was about to laugh at me or anything, but like he was entertained. My eyes traveled along the long lashes behind his glasses to the curve of his cheek to the jut of his jaw.

Rin closed the book and looked up at me. "I love these!"

"Really?"

"Not quite what I expected," Rin said. "These are sweet and funny and kawaii."

He used the Japanese word for "cute." "Oh, I get it. And I'm none of those things." I smiled to let him know I was joking.

He smiled back. "You're *all* those things."

My heart hammered.

"So, Sakai," Rin started.

"Call me Jenna. Please."

"Jenna." He said my name softly. My heart did a stupid skip. Maybe I needed to go to the doctor to get it checked out. "Do you want to go with me to open mic night?"

"Ah, I can't."

His smile faded.

"Wait! I mean, yes, I want to go. I *am* going. But I'm already getting a ride there with my friend."

"Isabella?" Rin asked.

"Yeah."

"Can we hang out after? Tate can give you a ride home."

"Sure. Okay."

"It's a date, then."

"A date?"

His eyes met mine, and he smiled. "A date."

A warmth spread through me and wrapped around me like a blanket. And then another thought popped into my head, and before I could smack it away, I let the words come tumbling out of my mouth. "Do you want to meet my friends?"

He lifted an eyebrow. Adorable.

"I was thinking of inviting them here tomorrow. If that's okay."

"That sounds good."

Humming to himself, Rin opened his sketchbook and started drawing, and I did the same. But I couldn't doodle any of my usual things. My pen seemed to have a mind of its own as I drew happy face after happy face. At least I didn't draw any silly hearts. I turned to a fresh page before Rin saw what I was doing, but when I peeked up at him, he was watching me.

And smiling.

Thirty-six

"Dude, this banana shake is...bananas!" Doug said, shooting a straw wrapper across the crowded booth.

Conner retaliated with his own straw wrapper, nailing Doug between the eyes, making the guys burst out laughing.

Teddy bit into his hamburger, juice running down his chin. Keiko passed him a napkin and returned to drinking her Chocolate Shake Where It Happens. Leigh had outdone herself today with songs for each of the orders. Everyone had burst into spontaneous applause without any prompting.

Like we had every day since my friends started

joining us at the diner, Rin and I sat in the middle of our corner booth, our knees pressed against each other. Keiko, Conner, and Teddy were wedged in next to me. On the opposite side, Isabella nibbled on non-cheesy Fetch Fries while Doug nursed his shake, the two of them excitedly talking about a new *Battle of the Bands* video game.

"I don't think you two will ever have this booth to yourselves again," Keiko told me.

"I think you're right," I said with a happy smile. After I'd invited everyone to hang at the diner, they'd started showing up regularly after basketball. Isabella and I walked here after newspaper club.

I reached across Rin's sketchbook to grab a fry, but before I could, he took my hand and wrapped his fingers around mine. I glanced at him, but he just kept drawing with his left hand. I could barely believe it when he placed our joined hands on the table between us. In front of everybody. Keiko grinned at me, waggling her eyebrows. I used my free hand to snag the last Fetch Fry from the plate we were sharing.

It was nice to be surrounded by my friends. Rin still sketched in his book, and to everyone's delight, he started drawing manga characters of them.

Tomorrow he was coming over to my dad's place. We'd decided to work on a manga together. Not for anyone else but ourselves. Sometimes it was okay to just do things for fun.

And sometimes you needed to follow through. I'd sent my scholarship application entry to Ms. Fontes just in time to meet the deadline. It had taken me a long time to find the story I wanted to tell. It wasn't about winning or digging up dirt or proving anything. But it was about exposing the truth. My personal truth.

And I thought it was a pretty good story.

Lessons from Heartbreak
By Jenna Sakai

Heartbreak is for suckers. That was my motto, and I swore by it. Until I didn't.

My family is good at building walls. Instead of talking about things that matter, we spent most of my life talking around them. Each word we didn't say was a brick stacked between us. And we built those walls up until there was no way to get through them.

When I was nine years old, my parents stopped

loving each other. They yelled and screamed and fought. All the time. When I was eleven, they got a divorce. My dad moved halfway across the country. And my mom didn't yell anymore, but she didn't talk much either—at least not about anything that mattered.

I was so angry that I did exactly what I'd seen them do a hundred times. I built a wall around myself to keep them—and everyone else in the world—from ever hurting me again. I thought I didn't need anyone. That caring only led to pain. That facts were safer than feelings.

That was part of the reason I want to be an investigative reporter. I love solving a puzzle, doing my research, and if I'm honest, being a little nosy. I admire the journalist's sense of objectivity and communicating the unbiased truth. But I thought being objective meant not having feelings. I've recently learned that I wasn't objective at all. Not about my parents or my classmates or the exposé I was planning on entering in this competition. I had preconceived opinions about almost everything, and none of them were good. I let those judgmental opinions color my thoughts and affect the stories that I wrote. Worse, I pushed everyone in my life away.

Lately I've been hiding at a diner not far from school. When I first discovered it, I thought it was just about perfect because it was mostly empty and nobody I knew went there. I could sit in my booth, alone, eat junk food, and work on all the articles I wanted to write and the truths I wanted to tell. But then, one day, someone snuck into my booth. And he had just as many walls built up as I did. The more I got to know him, the more I realized that being alone can be really lonely. And that making assumptions instead of talking about what's really going on doesn't help anyone.

But my walls are starting to crumble. I'm lucky to have a lot of people in my life who care about me. My best friend is patient when I'm being stubborn. My dad—who moved back to town recently— listened when my anger at him finally blew up, and we shared the first honest conversation we've had, maybe ever. My mom sees how hard things have been for me and is making small changes in her attitude that make a big difference. I have teachers who want me to be the best version of myself I can be, whatever that looks like. My friends make me laugh, get me to try new things, and tell me when I'm wrong. And that guy from the diner? He's turning into someone very special to me. All these people have been chipping away at my defenses without me even realizing it.

Now it's up to me to do the hardest work. I'm trying my best to demolish the walls, brick by brick, word by word. It's going to take time, but I'm learning. And I'm going to start by letting myself feel every sad, angry, joyful, anxious, scary feeling I have. It's the only way I'll ever become the person I want to be—a good daughter, a good friend, and hopefully a good writer.

Heartbreak isn't for suckers. It only means that I have a heart to break. I thought I needed walls to protect mine because it was fragile. But my heart is way sturdier than I ever thought.

I don't need walls. Yes, letting people in means risking heartbreak. It takes courage. But I'm strong enough to handle it.

acknowledgments

As someone who had a long road to publication, I am familiar with heartbreak. Fortunately, I am blessed with an amazing community.

This book would not have been possible without my awesome editor, Jenne Abramowitz—thank you for asking for a sequel to *Keep It Together, Keiko Carter* and for being excited about a companion novel. Thank you also for your guidance in making this a much better book. You took my words and helped me blend them into a delicious shake of a story. You get me. You really get me!

To Tricia Lawrence, thank you for believing in my work and in me. You are a superb agent, fabulous NYC travel companion, and wonderful friend. Let's keep making dreams come true!

To trusted readers for insightful feedback, thank you Andrea Wang, Kristy Boyce, Jasmine Perry, Cindy Faughnan, and Jo Knowles—you all make me a better writer. Much gratitude to cheerleaders Josie Cameron, Jason June, Daphne Benedis-Grab, and Susan Tan for talking me off ledges. Big hugs to my EMLA family. Special thanks to Leigh Bauer for sharing her knowledge of Broadway shows and all things teen.

I am overjoyed to be part of the Scholastic family. A warm thank-you to the Sakai squad, including Shelly Romero, Abby McAden, Jordana Kulak, Rachel Feld, Julia Eisler, Josh Berlowitz, Janell Harris, Nikki Mutch, and the whole sales team—your support and assistance mean the world to me. For the fabulous cover and book design, thank you Stephanie Yang, Yaffa Jaskoll, photographer Michael Frost, and cover model Zoe Manarel.

To everyone who loved Keiko Carter, thank you for reading and sharing. Thank you, Alexandra Devlin at RightsPeople for foreign sales. Big thanks to Dennis Stephens, bon vivant at EMLA, for all you do. Much appreciation to my friends and the kidlit community, with a special shout-out to the Asian community for letting me know how much it means to see yourselves/your readers reflected in my stories. Gratitude to the Highlights Foundation and SCBWI, and to Sara Zarr and Jenn Laughran for friendship and encouragement when I was starting out. To teachers, librarians, and booksellers everywhere, thank you for putting books into readers' hands.

While Jenna wasn't willing to admit that her love for Japanese curry was in part sentimental, I am. Japanese curry reminds me of my late father, Denta Hirokane. Now I share the love of this dish with my daughter.

And always, a big thank-you to my family: my husband, Bob Florence; my daughter, Caitlin Masako Schumacher; my stepson, Jason Florence; my parents, Bob and Yasuko Fordiani; my sister and her family, Gail Hirokane, John Parkison, and Laurel Parkison; and the rest of my relatives and the Florence family for all the enthusiastic support. I love you all!

More friendship drama and first crushes
from Debbi Michiko Florence!

Best friends . . . forever?

Seventh grade is supposed to be a game changer. And Keiko thinks she's got it covered, especially with Audrey and Jenna by her side. But while she's been dreaming about triple dates, first kisses, and a boy she really shouldn't have a crush on, the friendship she's always thought was rock-solid is beginning to crumble.

How is Keiko supposed to keep it all together?

about the author

Debbi Michiko Florence is the author of *Keep It Together, Keiko Carter*, a Junior Library Guild Gold Standard Selection and New England Book Award finalist, and the Jasmine Toguchi chapter books. A third-generation Japanese American and native Californian, Debbi lives in Connecticut with her husband, rescue dog, rabbit, and duck. Visit her online at debbimichikoflorence.com.